MEMORABILIA

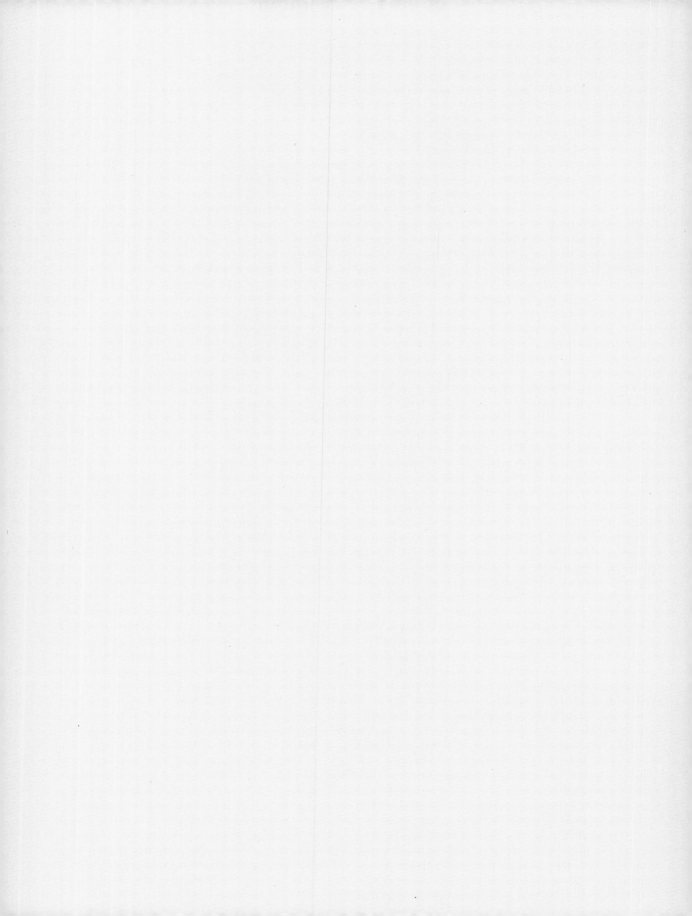

SERGIO PONCHIONE

MEMORABILIA

FANTAGRAPHICS BOOKS

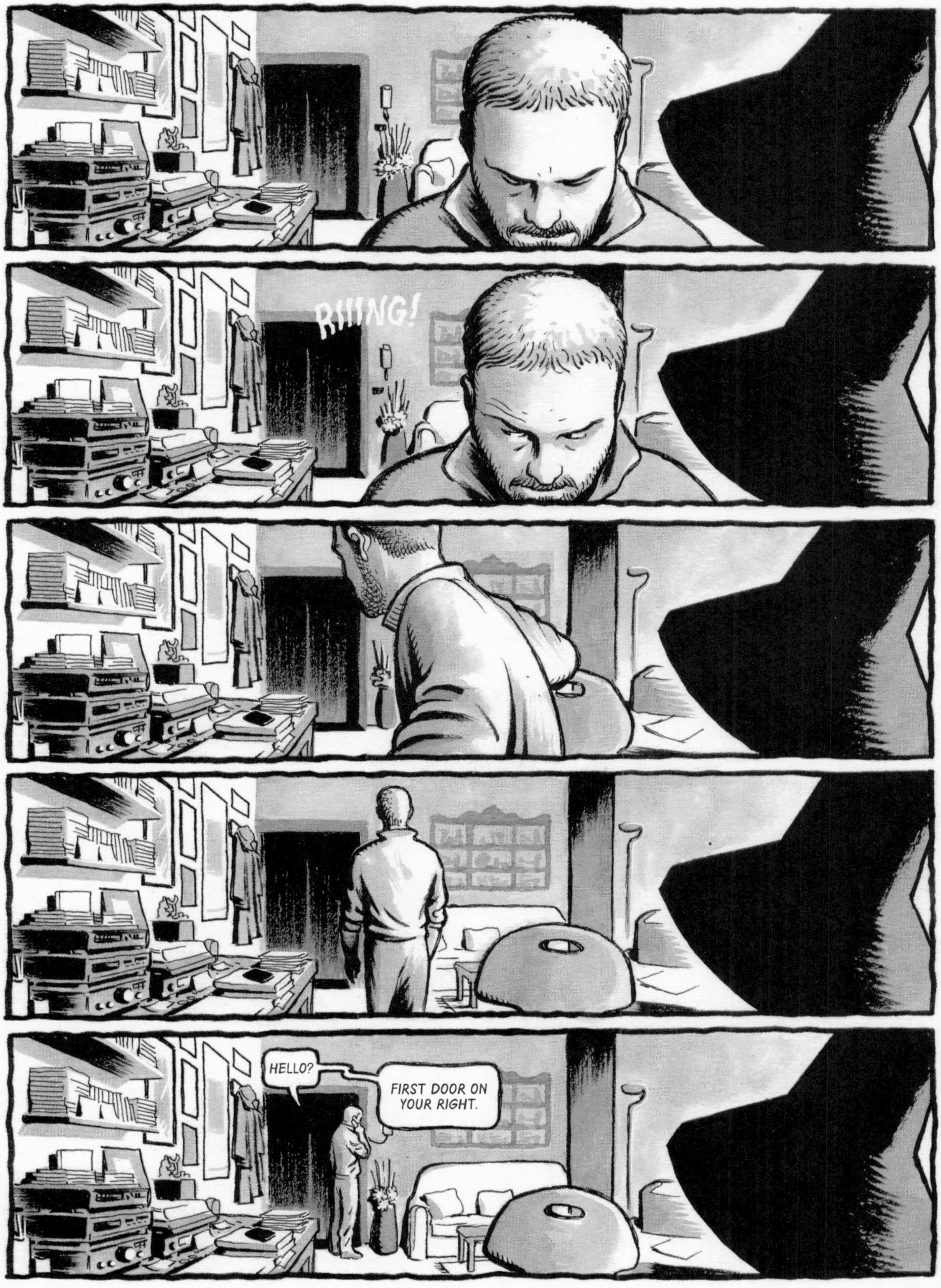
RIIING!
HELLO?
FIRST DOOR ON YOUR RIGHT.

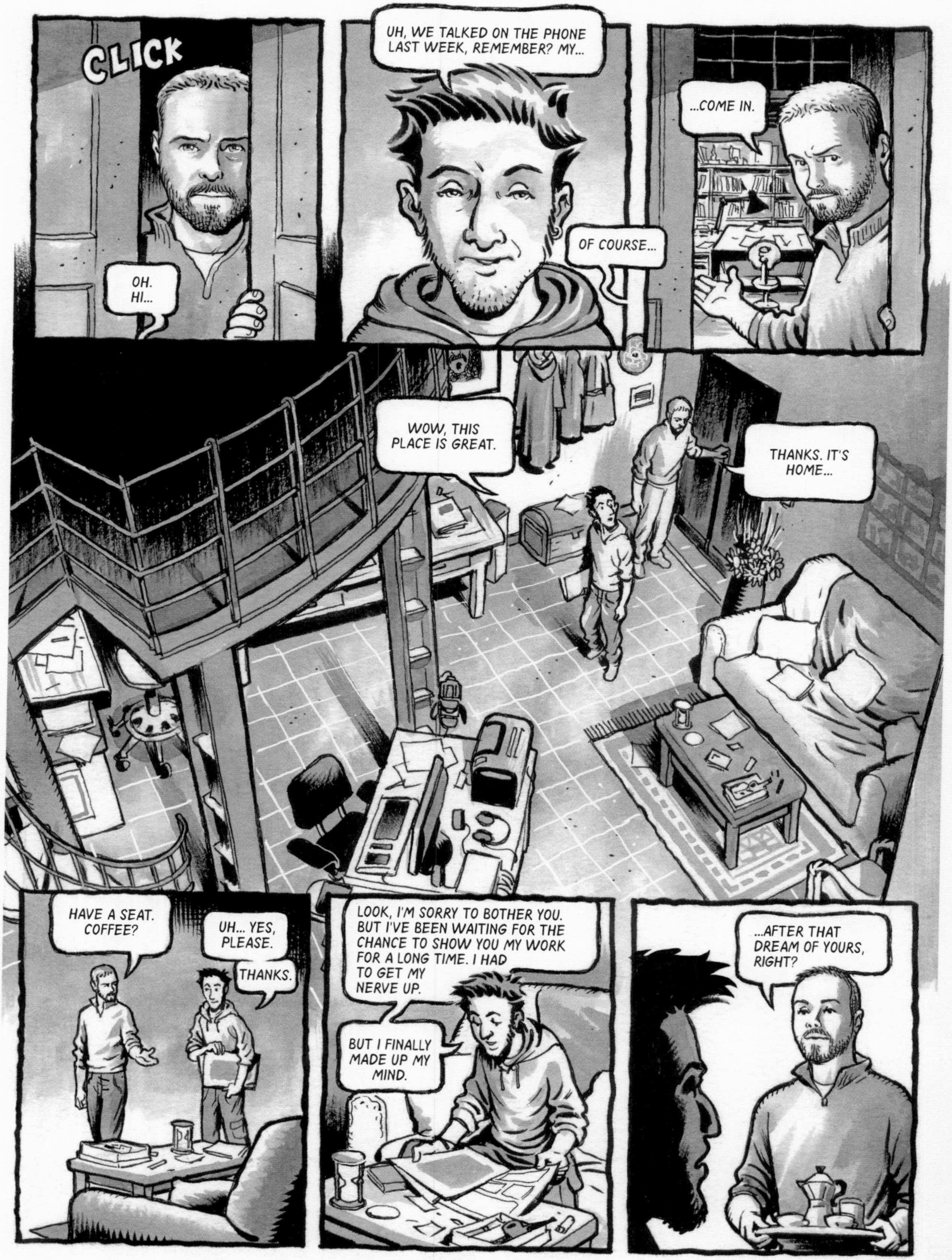
CLICK
OH. HI...
UH, WE TALKED ON THE PHONE LAST WEEK, REMEMBER? MY...
OF COURSE...
...COME IN.
WOW, THIS PLACE IS GREAT.
THANKS. IT'S HOME...
HAVE A SEAT. COFFEE?
UH... YES, PLEASE.
THANKS.
LOOK, I'M SORRY TO BOTHER YOU. BUT I'VE BEEN WAITING FOR THE CHANCE TO SHOW YOU MY WORK FOR A LONG TIME. I HAD TO GET MY NERVE UP.
BUT I FINALLY MADE UP MY MIND.
...AFTER THAT DREAM OF YOURS, RIGHT?

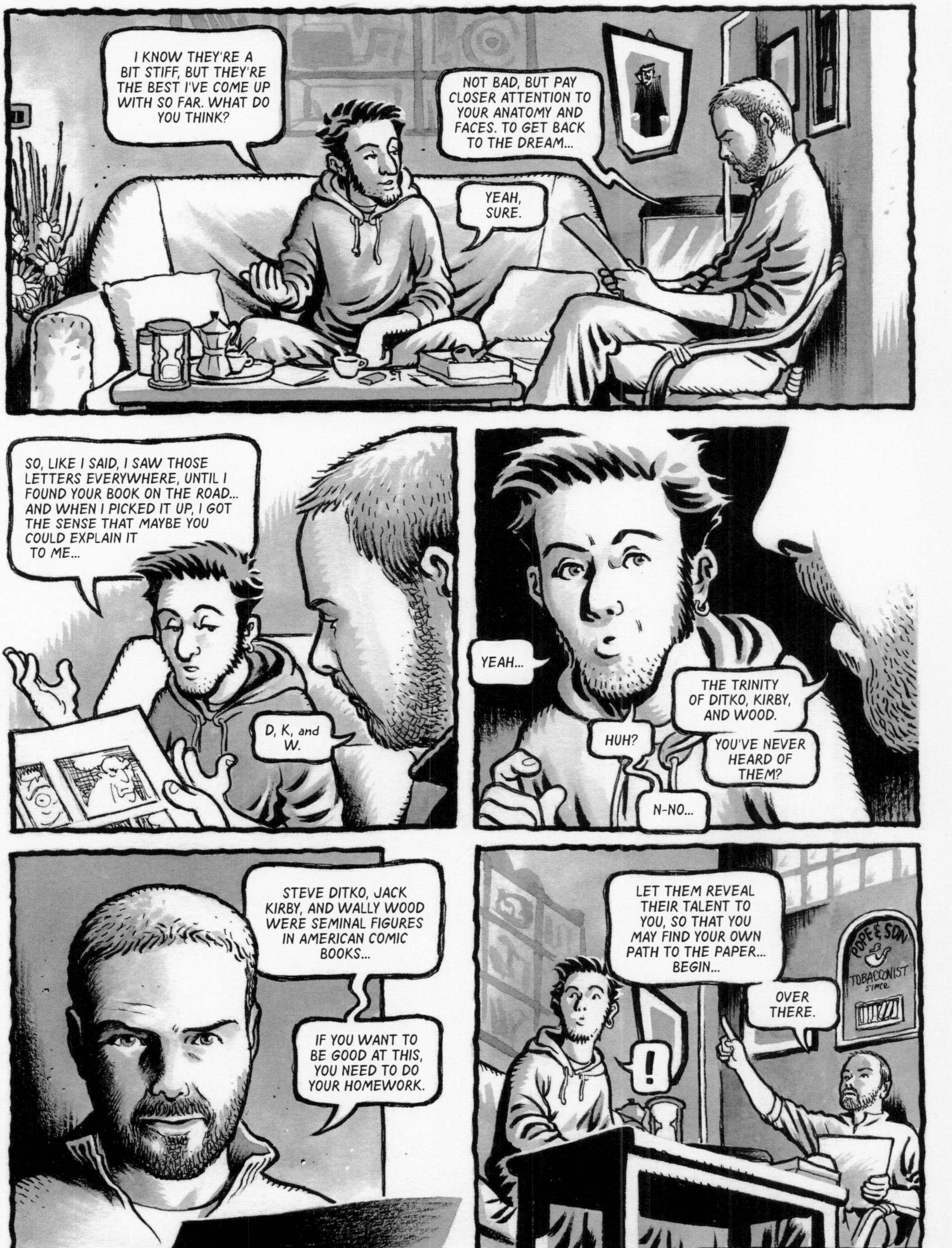
I KNOW THEY'RE A BIT STIFF, BUT THEY'RE THE BEST I'VE COME UP WITH SO FAR. WHAT DO YOU THINK?
NOT BAD, BUT PAY CLOSER ATTENTION TO YOUR ANATOMY AND FACES. TO GET BACK TO THE DREAM...
YEAH, SURE.
SO, LIKE I SAID, I SAW THOSE LETTERS EVERYWHERE, UNTIL I FOUND YOUR BOOK ON THE ROAD... AND WHEN I PICKED IT UP, I GOT THE SENSE THAT MAYBE YOU COULD EXPLAIN IT TO ME...
D, K, and W.
YEAH...
THE TRINITY OF DITKO, KIRBY, AND WOOD.
HUH?
YOU'VE NEVER HEARD OF THEM?
N-NO...
STEVE DITKO, JACK KIRBY, AND WALLY WOOD WERE SEMINAL FIGURES IN AMERICAN COMIC BOOKS...
IF YOU WANT TO BE GOOD AT THIS, YOU NEED TO DO YOUR HOMEWORK.
LET THEM REVEAL THEIR TALENT TO YOU, SO THAT YOU MAY FIND YOUR OWN PATH TO THE PAPER... BEGIN...
!
OVER THERE.
POPE & SON
TOBACCONIST
since

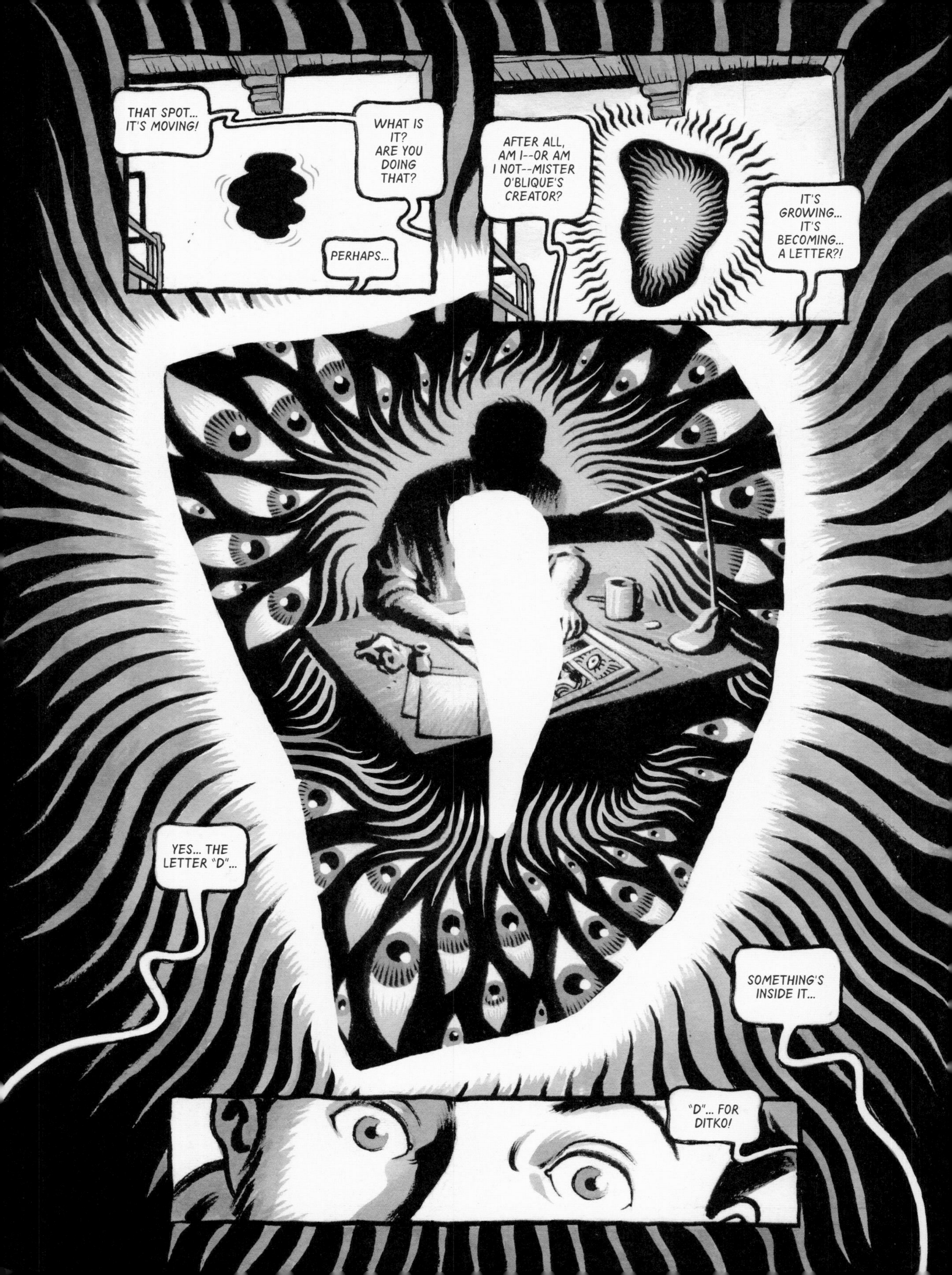

THAT SPOT... IT'S MOVING!
WHAT IS IT? ARE YOU DOING THAT?
PERHAPS...
AFTER ALL, AM I--OR AM I NOT--MISTER O'BLIQUE'S CREATOR?
IT'S GROWING... IT'S BECOMING... A LETTER?!
YES... THE LETTER "D"...
SOMETHING'S INSIDE IT...
"D"... FOR DITKO!

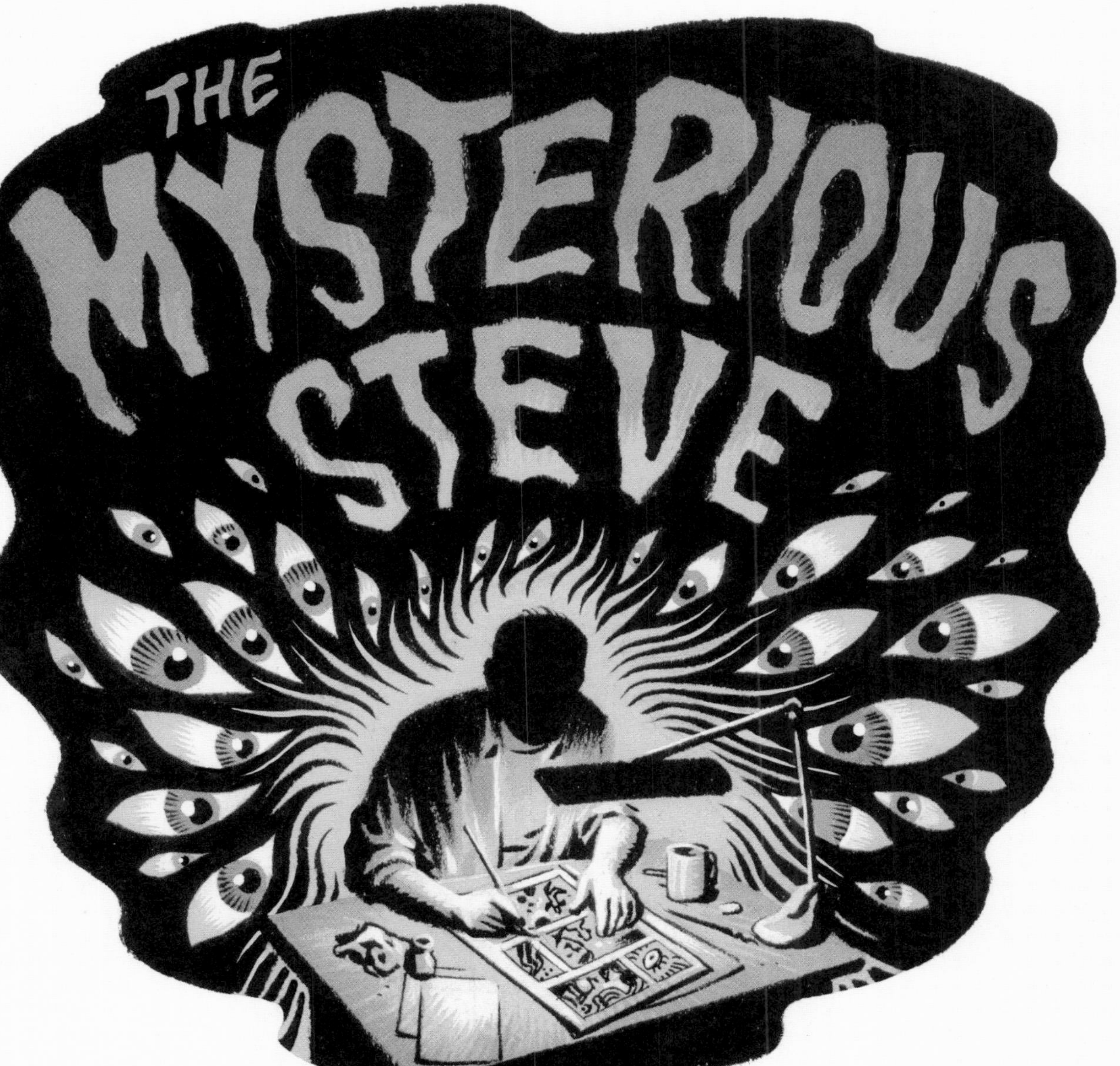
THE MYSTERIOUS STEVE

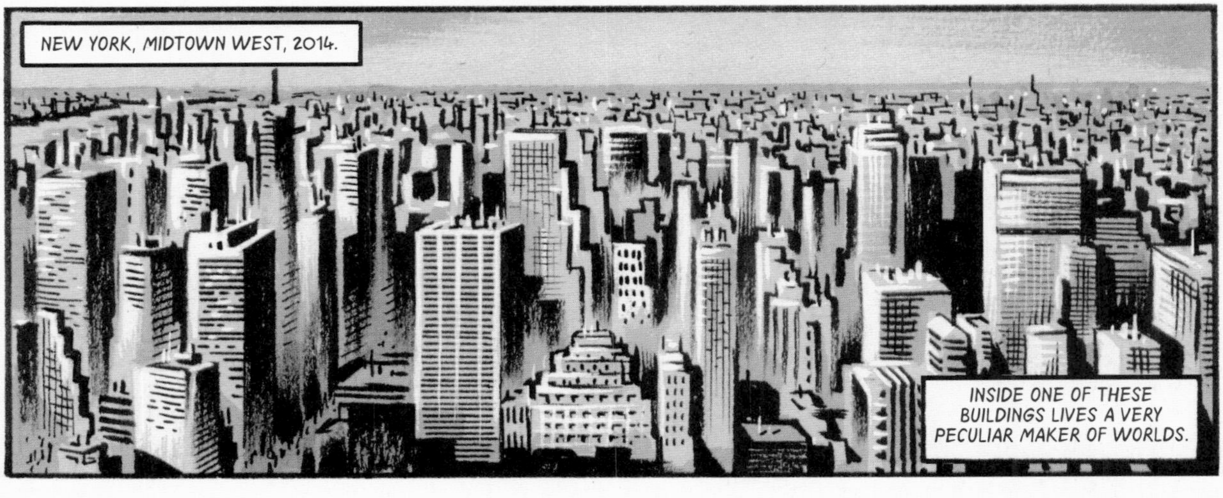
NEW YORK, MIDTOWN WEST, 2014.
INSIDE ONE OF THESE BUILDINGS LIVES A VERY PECULIAR MAKER OF WORLDS.

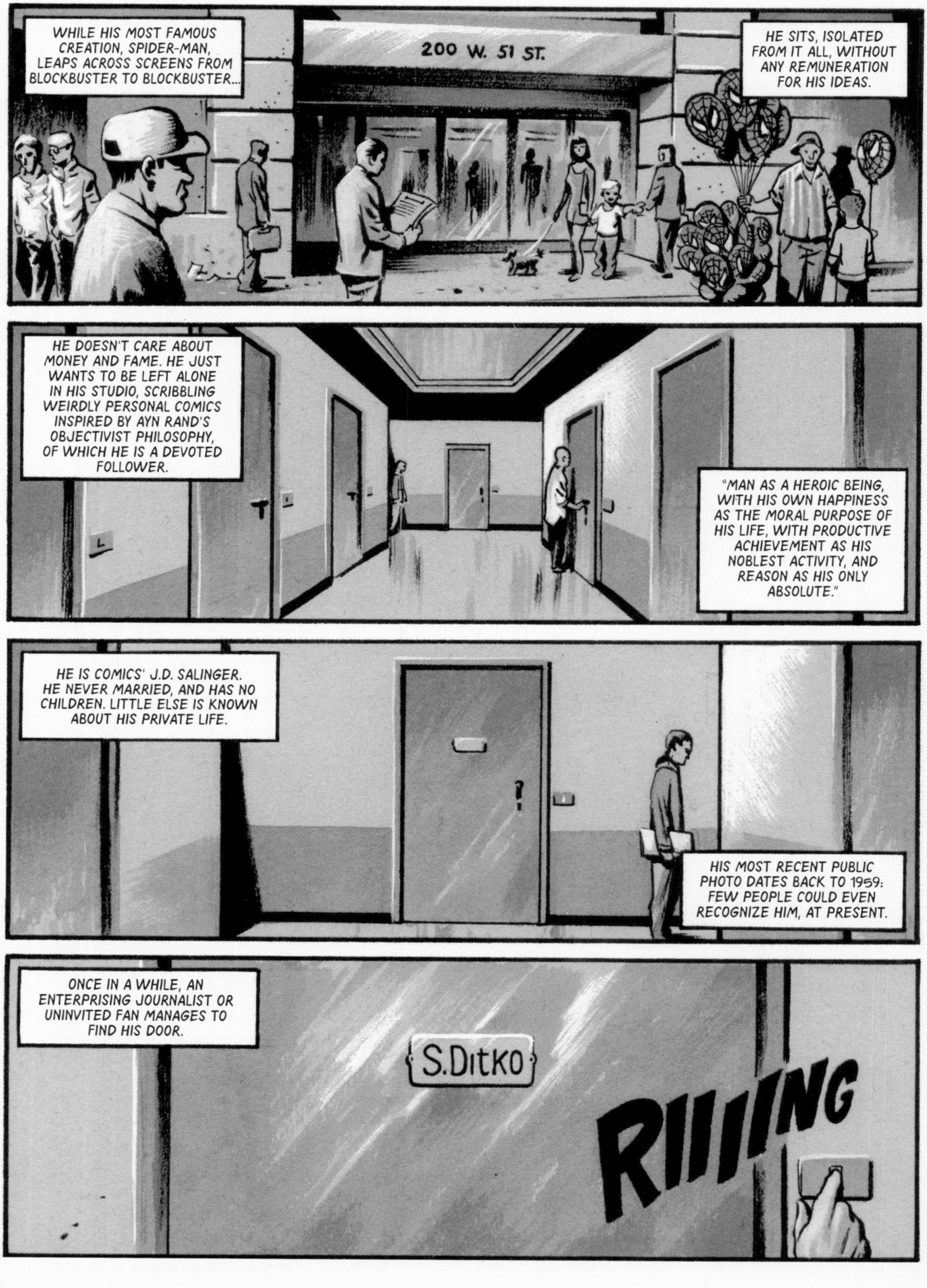
WHILE HIS MOST FAMOUS CREATION, SPIDER-MAN, LEAPS ACROSS SCREENS FROM BLOCKBUSTER TO BLOCKBUSTER...
200 W. 51 ST.
HE SITS, ISOLATED FROM IT ALL, WITHOUT ANY REMUNERATION FOR HIS IDEAS.
HE DOESN'T CARE ABOUT MONEY AND FAME. HE JUST WANTS TO BE LEFT ALONE IN HIS STUDIO, SCRIBBLING WEIRDLY PERSONAL COMICS INSPIRED BY AYN RAND'S OBJECTIVIST PHILOSOPHY, OF WHICH HE IS A DEVOTED FOLLOWER.
"MAN AS A HEROIC BEING, WITH HIS OWN HAPPINESS AS THE MORAL PURPOSE OF HIS LIFE, WITH PRODUCTIVE ACHIEVEMENT AS HIS NOBLEST ACTIVITY, AND REASON AS HIS ONLY ABSOLUTE."
HE IS COMICS' J.D. SALINGER. HE NEVER MARRIED, AND HAS NO CHILDREN. LITTLE ELSE IS KNOWN ABOUT HIS PRIVATE LIFE.
HIS MOST RECENT PUBLIC PHOTO DATES BACK TO 1959: FEW PEOPLE COULD EVEN RECOGNIZE HIM, AT PRESENT.
ONCE IN A WHILE, AN ENTERPRISING JOURNALIST OR UNINVITED FAN MANAGES TO FIND HIS DOOR.
S.DitkO
RIIIING

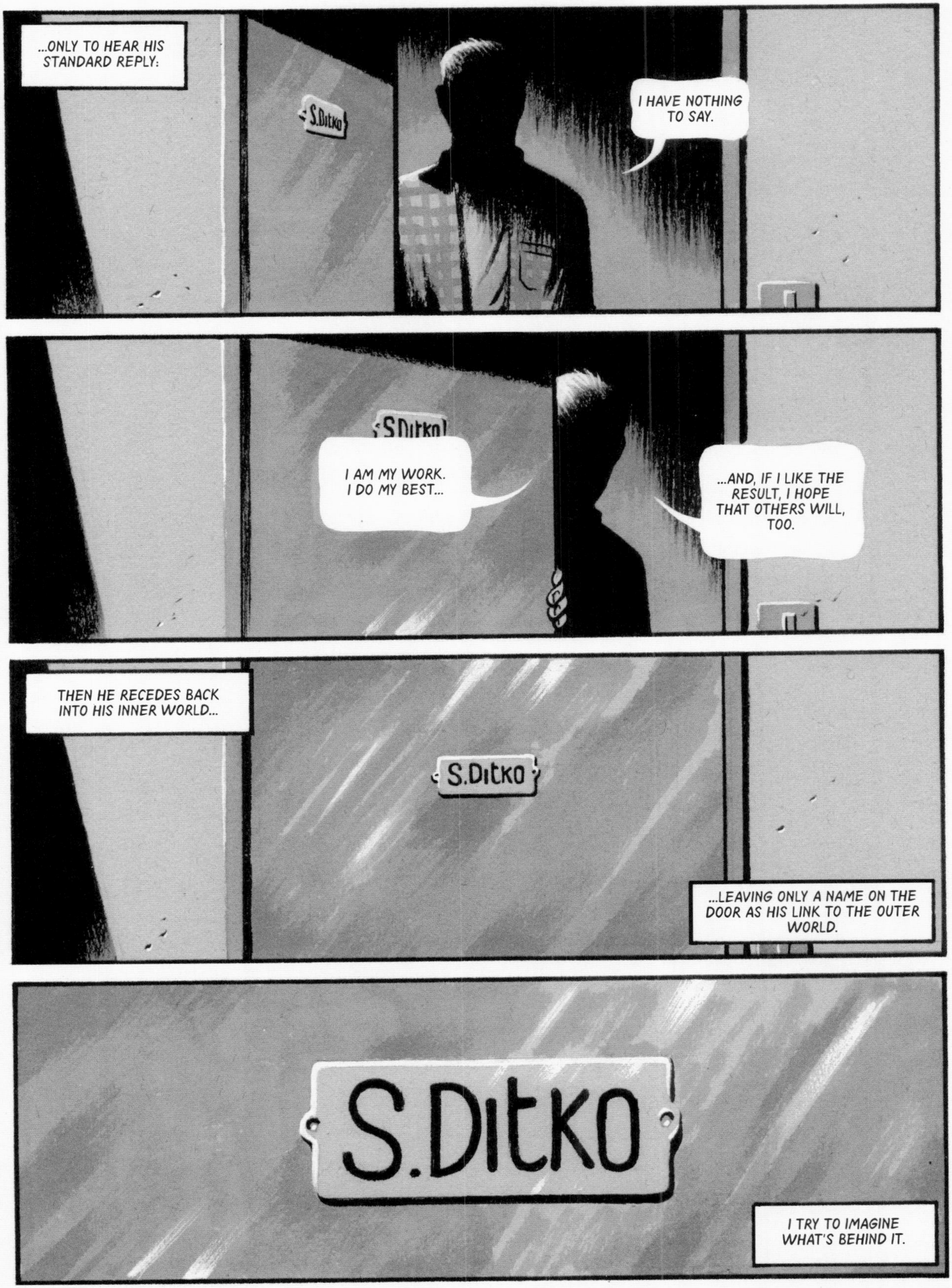
...ONLY TO HEAR HIS STANDARD REPLY:
S.Ditko
I HAVE NOTHING TO SAY.
S.Ditko
I AM MY WORK. I DO MY BEST...
...AND, IF I LIKE THE RESULT, I HOPE THAT OTHERS WILL, TOO.
THEN HE RECEDES BACK INTO HIS INNER WORLD...
S.Ditko
...LEAVING ONLY A NAME ON THE DOOR AS HIS LINK TO THE OUTER WORLD.
S.Ditko
I TRY TO IMAGINE WHAT'S BEHIND IT.

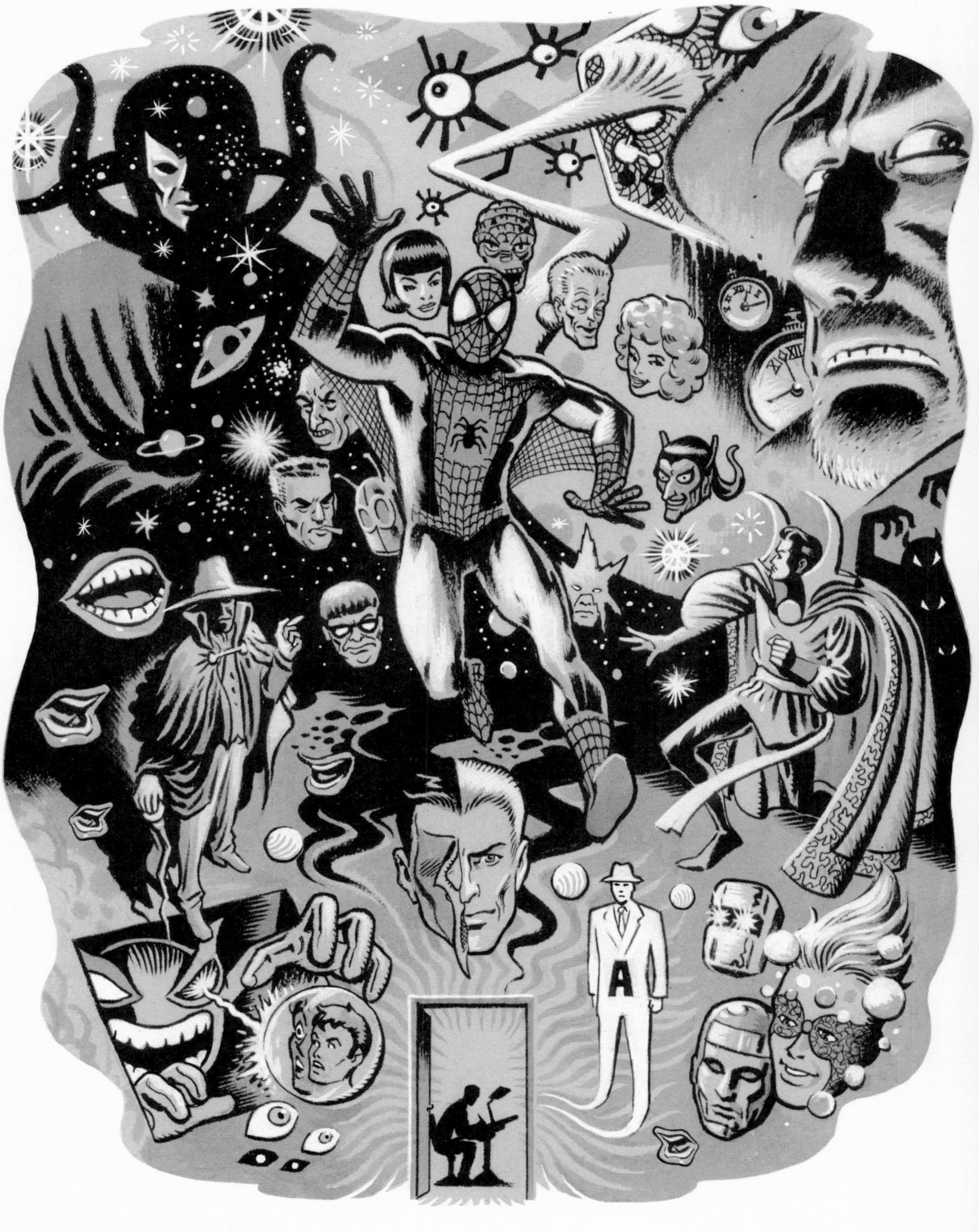

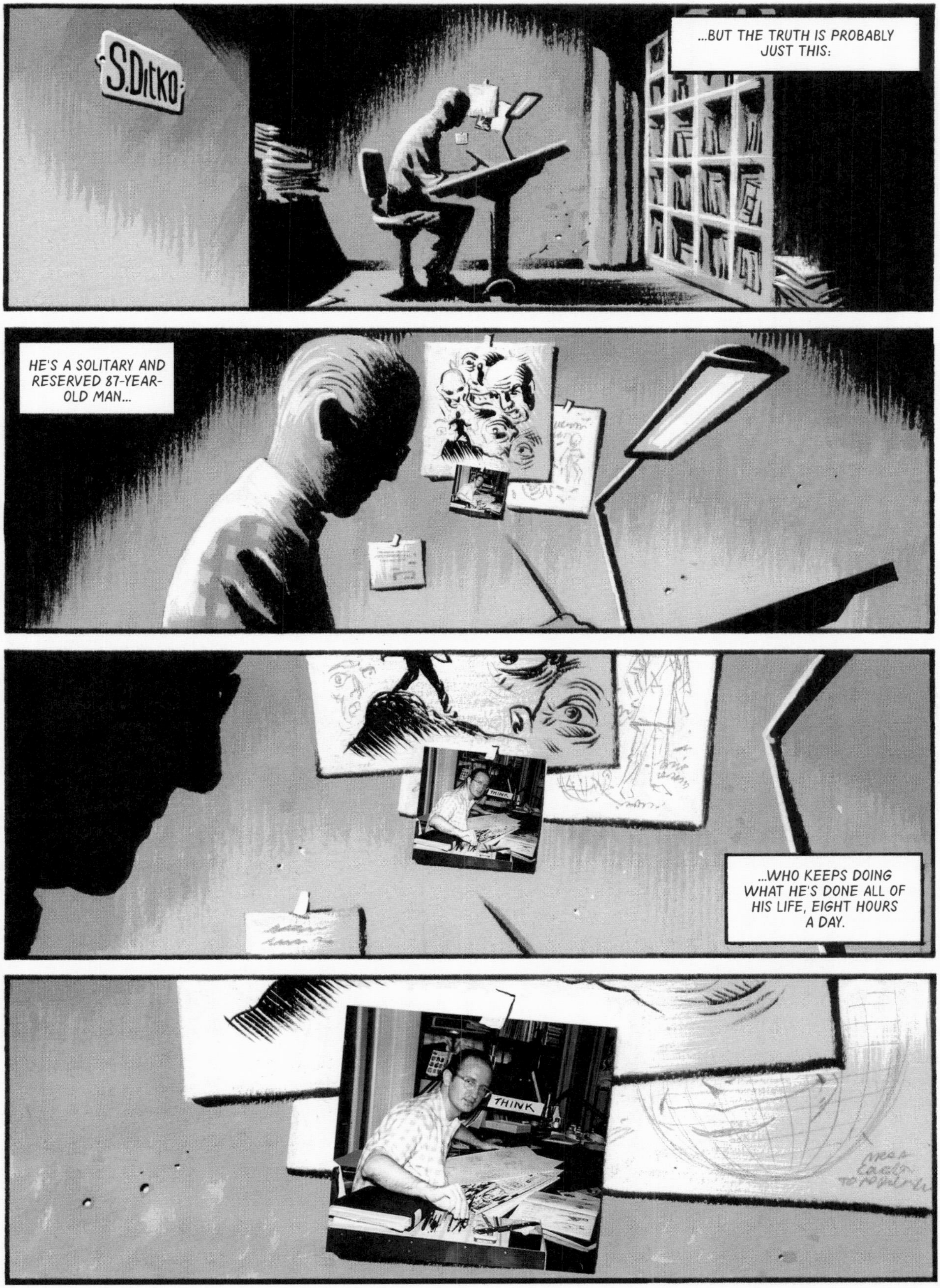
S.Ditko
...BUT THE TRUTH IS PROBABLY JUST THIS:
HE'S A SOLITARY AND RESERVED 87-YEAR-OLD MAN...
THINK
...WHO KEEPS DOING WHAT HE'S DONE ALL OF HIS LIFE, EIGHT HOURS A DAY.
THINK

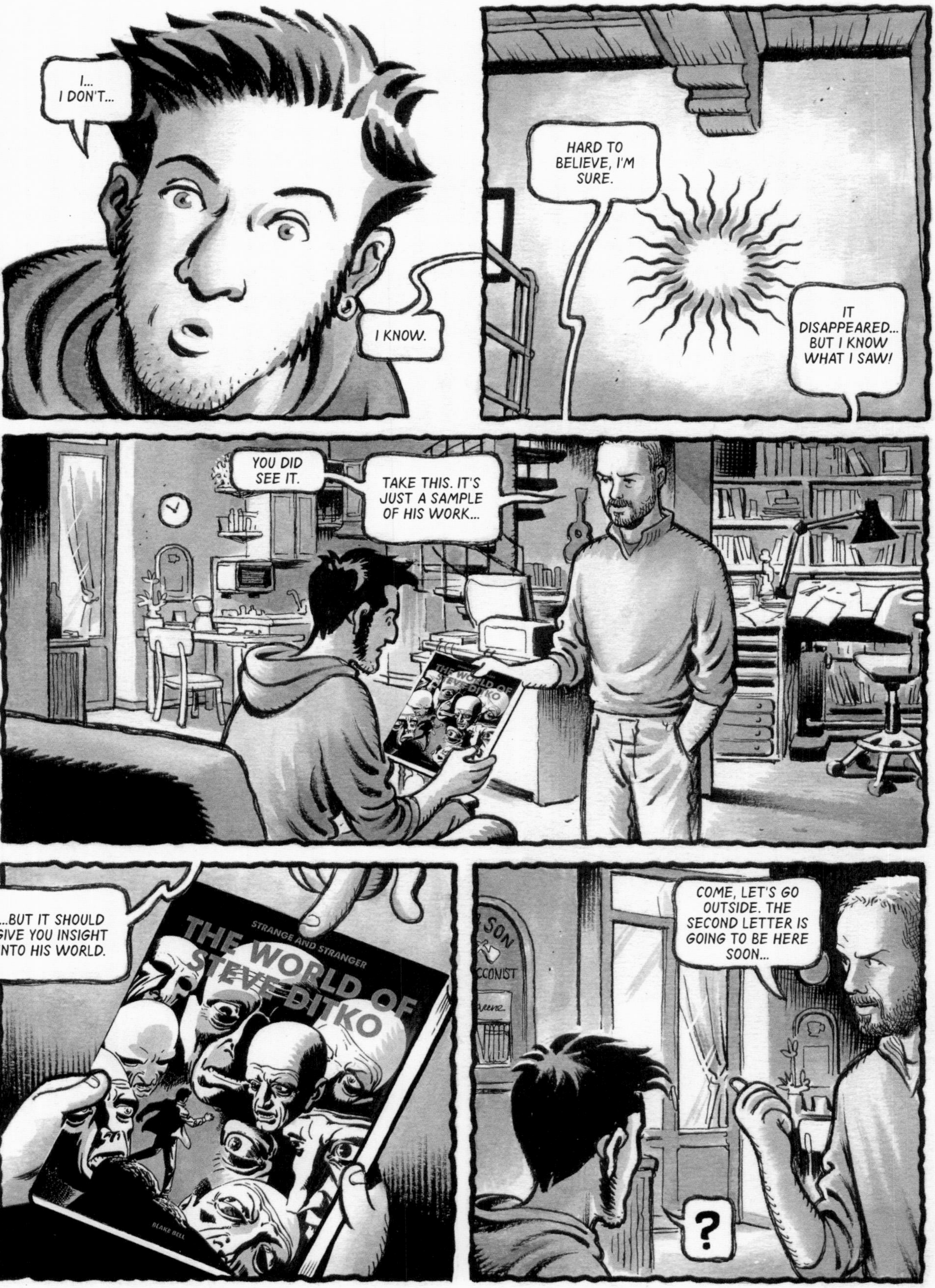
I... I DON'T...
I KNOW.
HARD TO BELIEVE, I'M SURE.
IT DISAPPEARED... BUT I KNOW WHAT I SAW!
YOU DID SEE IT.
TAKE THIS. IT'S JUST A SAMPLE OF HIS WORK...
THE WORLD OF STEVE DITKO
...BUT IT SHOULD GIVE YOU INSIGHT INTO HIS WORLD.
STRANGE AND STRANGER
THE WORLD OF STEVE DITKO
COME, LET'S GO OUTSIDE. THE SECOND LETTER IS GOING TO BE HERE SOON...
?

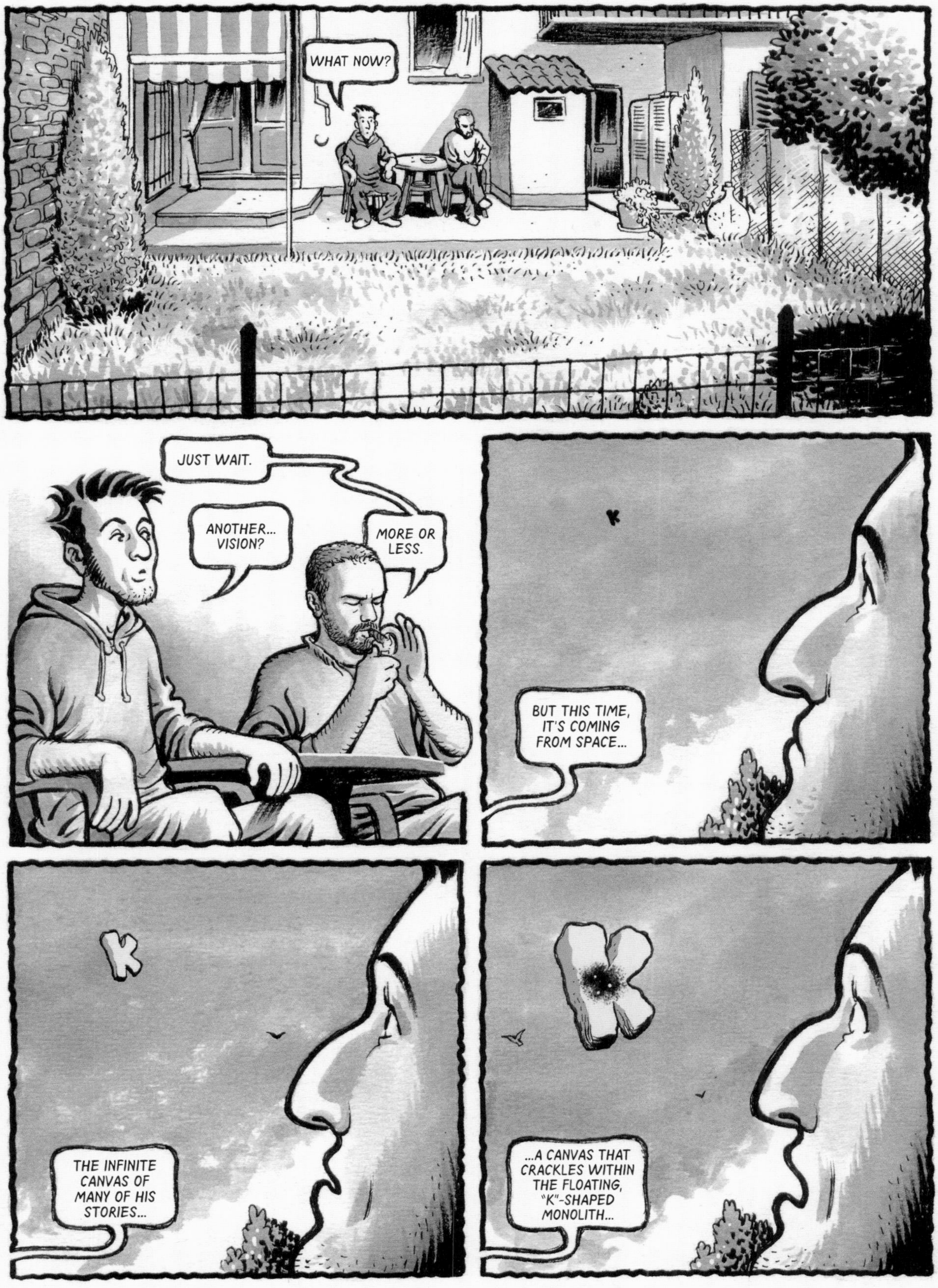
WHAT NOW?
JUST WAIT.
ANOTHER... VISION?
MORE OR LESS.
BUT THIS TIME, IT'S COMING FROM SPACE...
THE INFINITE CANVAS OF MANY OF HIS STORIES...
...A CANVAS THAT CRACKLES WITHIN THE FLOATING, "K"-SHAPED MONOLITH...

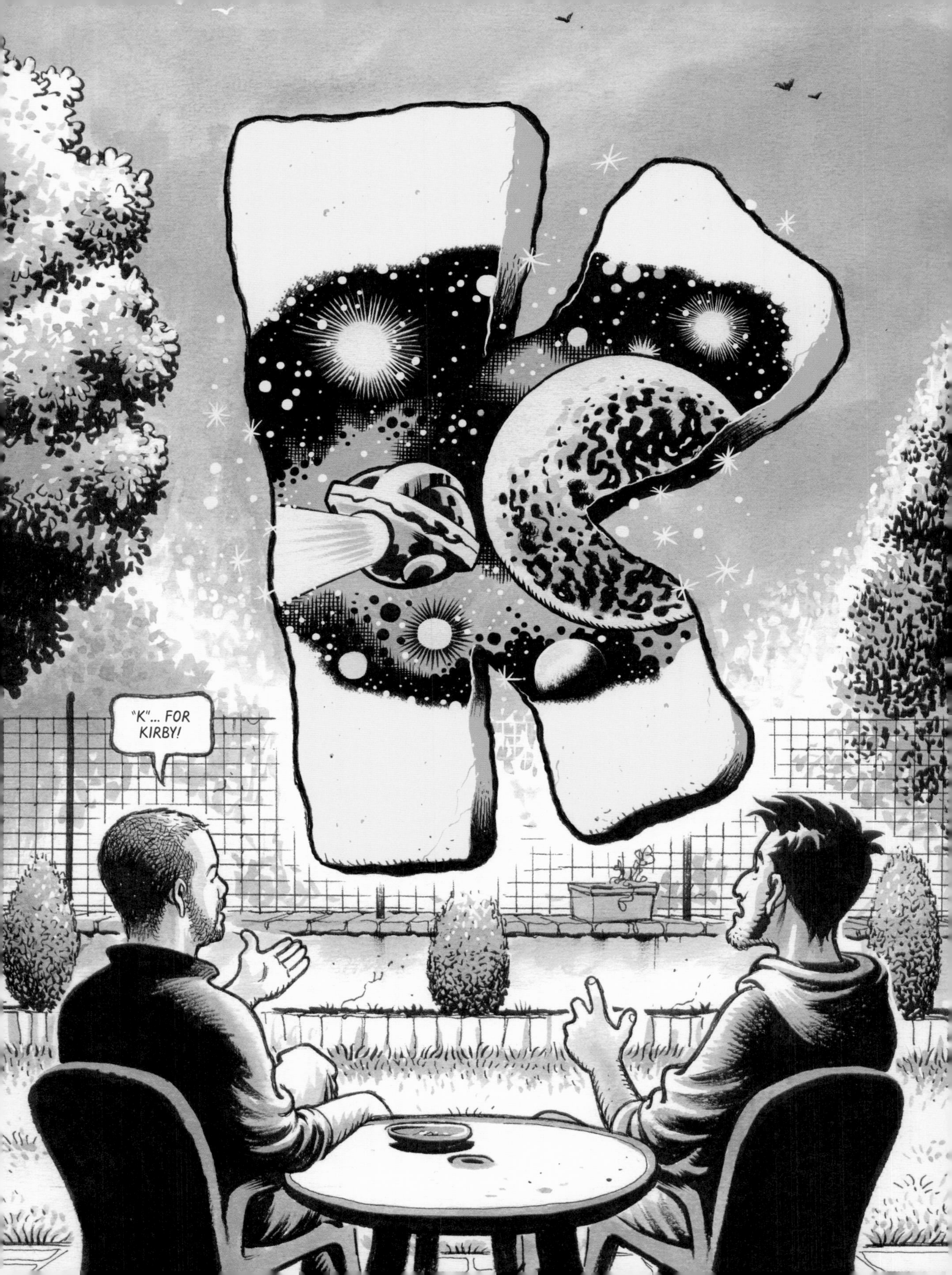
"K"... FOR KIRBY!

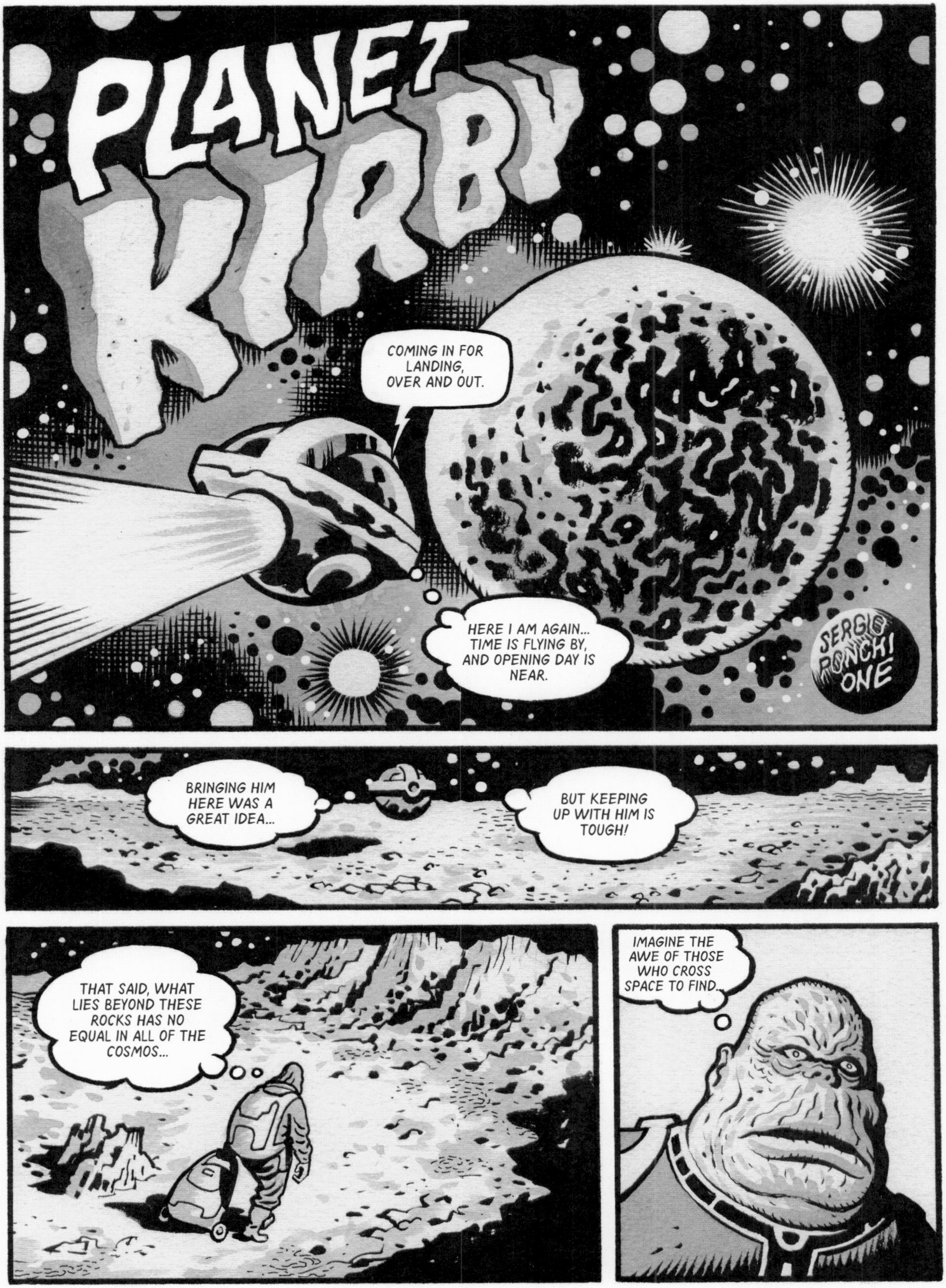

PLANET KIRBY
COMING IN FOR LANDING, OVER AND OUT.
HERE I AM AGAIN... TIME IS FLYING BY, AND OPENING DAY IS NEAR.
SERGIO PONCHIONE
BRINGING HIM HERE WAS A GREAT IDEA...
BUT KEEPING UP WITH HIM IS TOUGH!
THAT SAID, WHAT LIES BEYOND THESE ROCKS HAS NO EQUAL IN ALL OF THE COSMOS...
IMAGINE THE AWE OF THOSE WHO CROSS SPACE TO FIND...

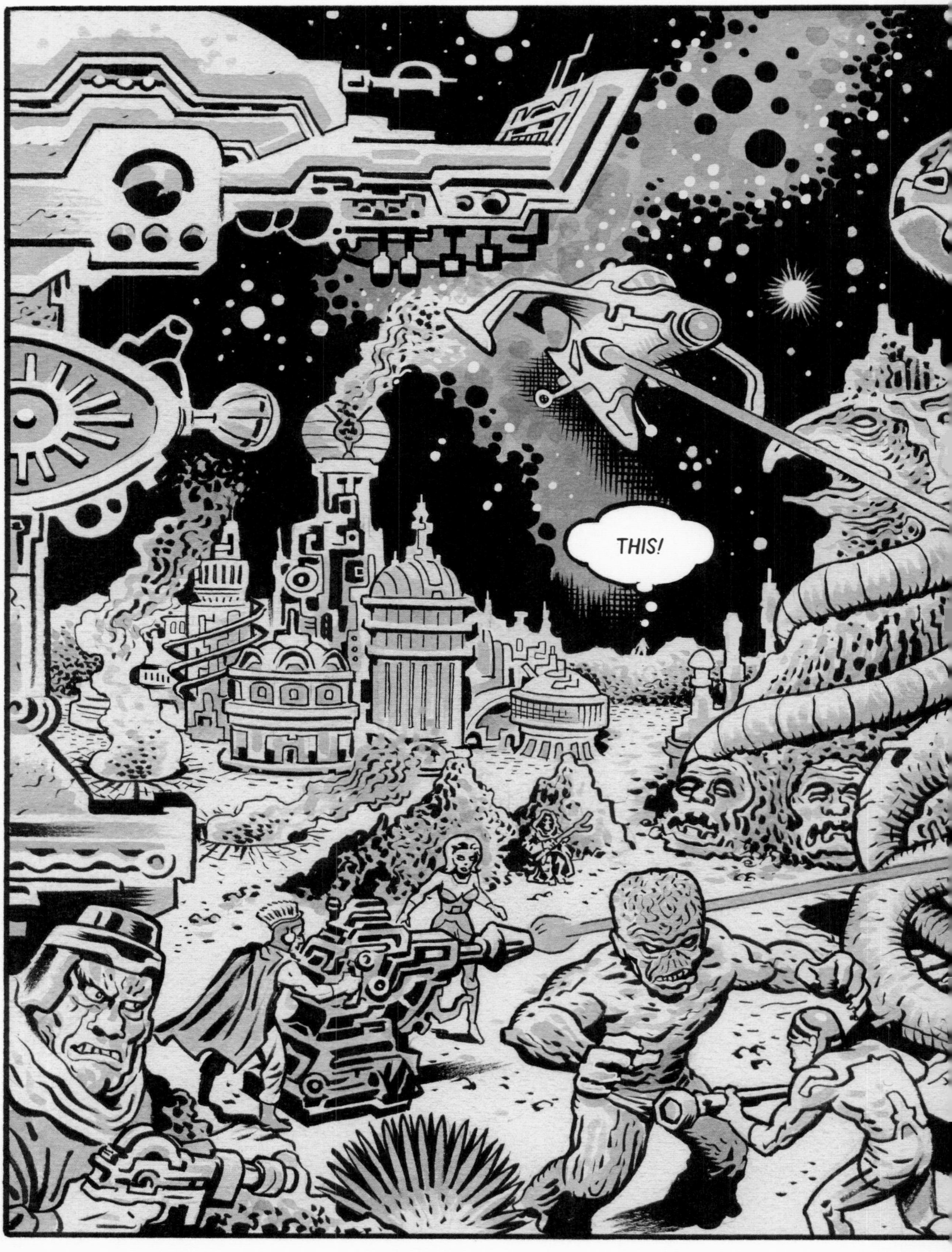
THIS!

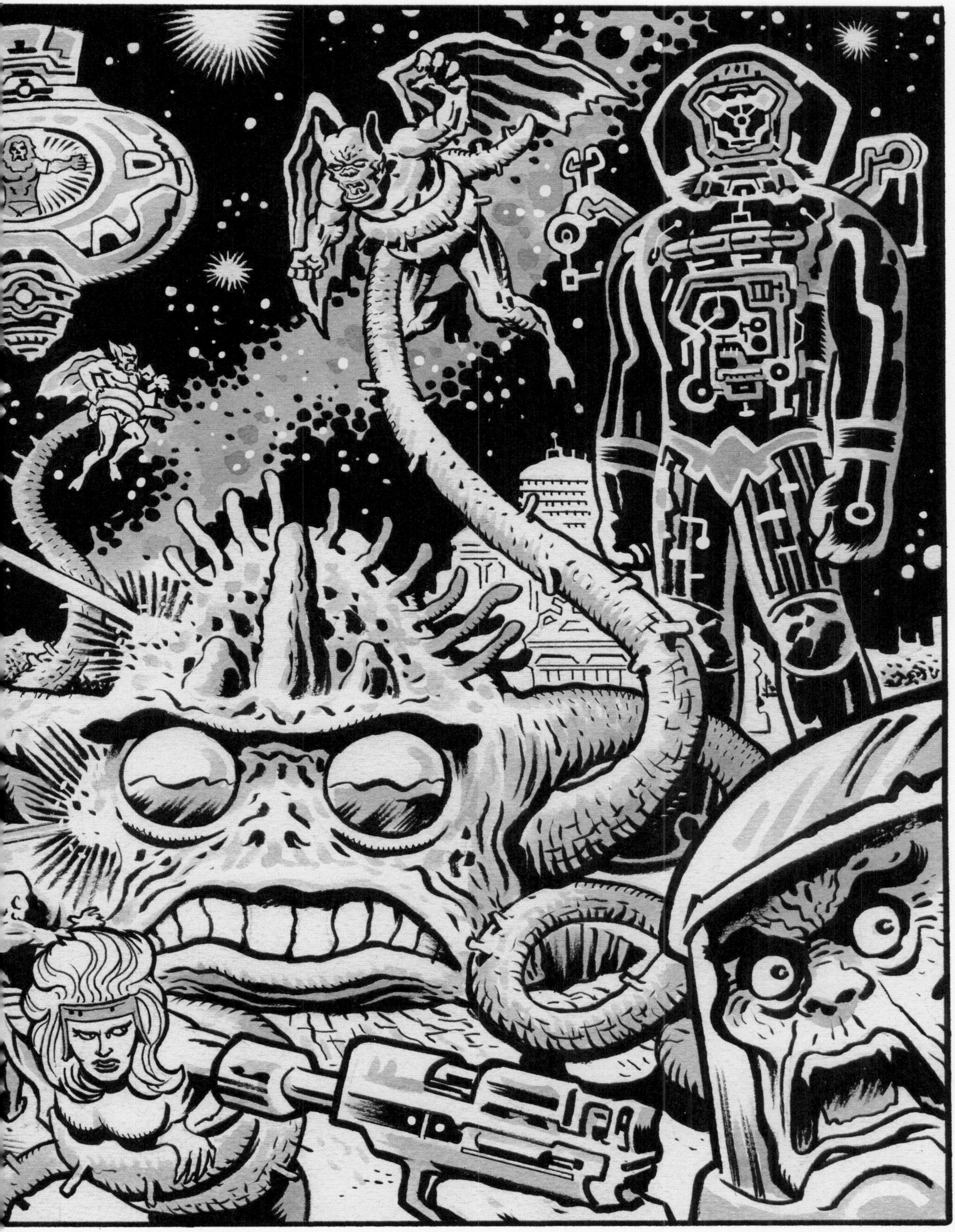

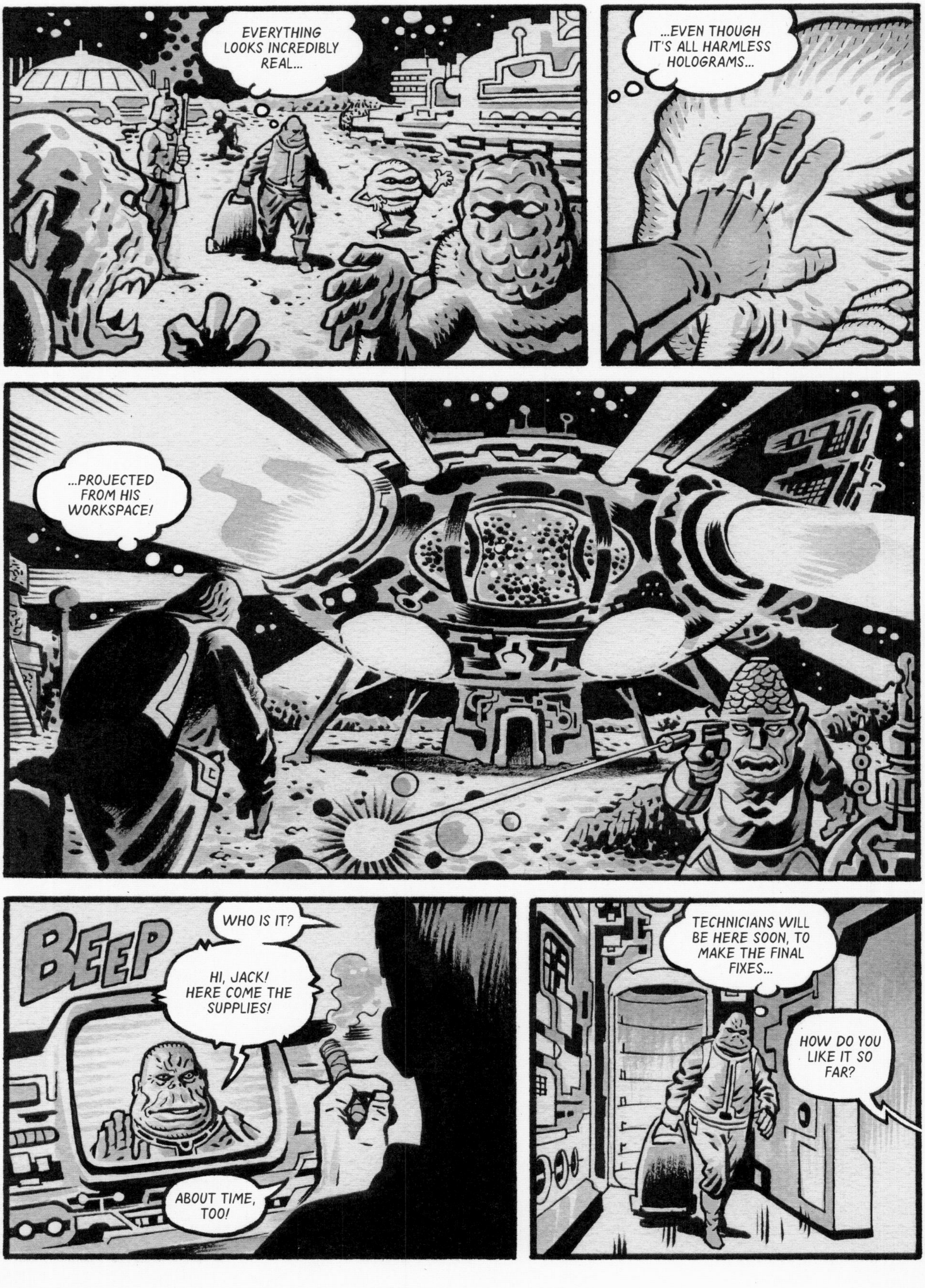
EVERYTHING LOOKS INCREDIBLY REAL...
...EVEN THOUGH IT'S ALL HARMLESS HOLOGRAMS...
...PROJECTED FROM HIS WORKSPACE!
BEEP
WHO IS IT?
HI, JACK! HERE COME THE SUPPLIES!
ABOUT TIME, TOO!
TECHNICIANS WILL BE HERE SOON, TO MAKE THE FINAL FIXES...
HOW DO YOU LIKE IT SO FAR?

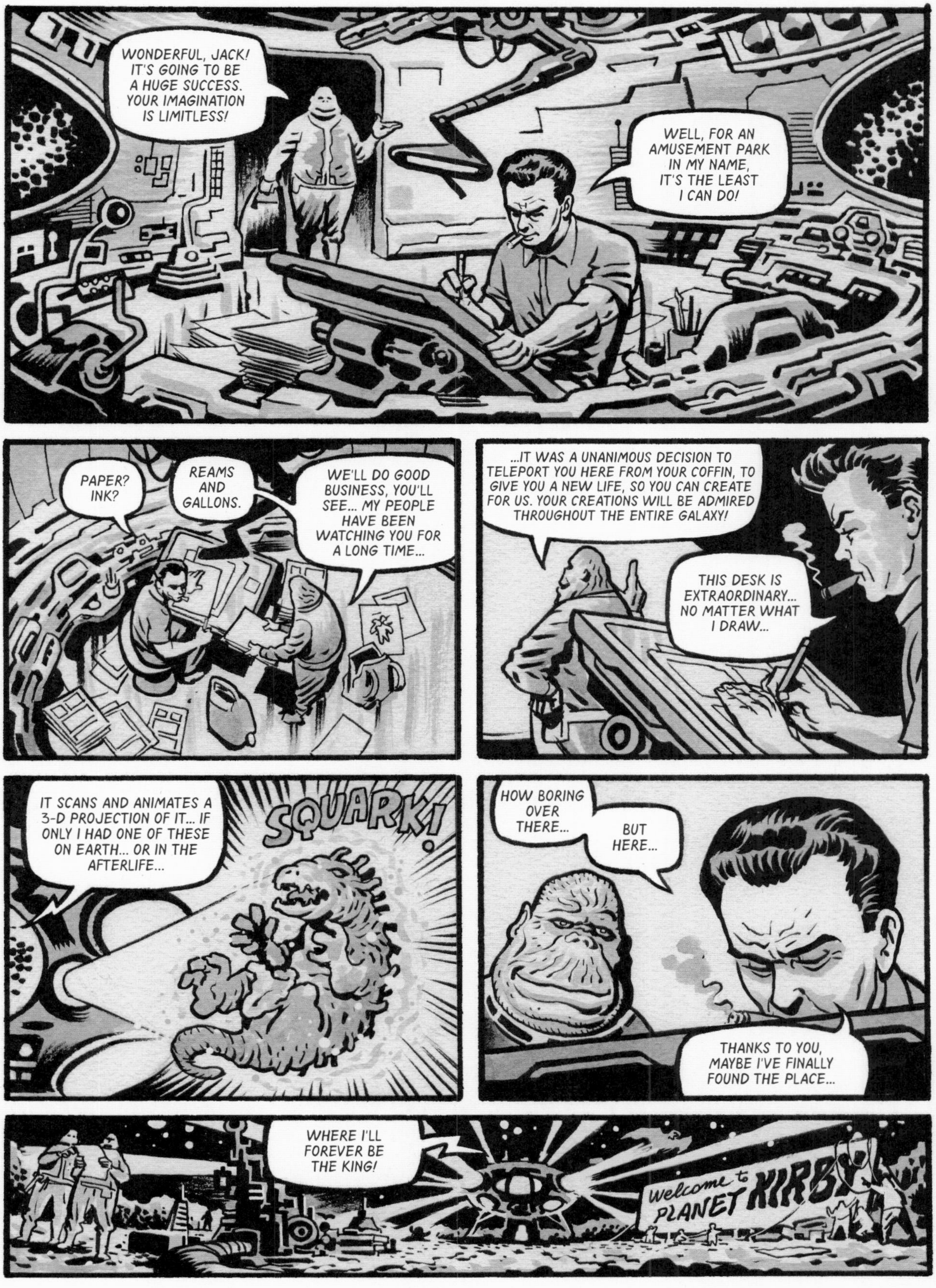
WONDERFUL, JACK! IT'S GOING TO BE A HUGE SUCCESS. YOUR IMAGINATION IS LIMITLESS!
WELL, FOR AN AMUSEMENT PARK IN MY NAME, IT'S THE LEAST I CAN DO!
PAPER? INK?
REAMS AND GALLONS.
WE'LL DO GOOD BUSINESS, YOU'LL SEE... MY PEOPLE HAVE BEEN WATCHING YOU FOR A LONG TIME...
...IT WAS A UNANIMOUS DECISION TO TELEPORT YOU HERE FROM YOUR COFFIN, TO GIVE YOU A NEW LIFE, SO YOU CAN CREATE FOR US. YOUR CREATIONS WILL BE ADMIRED THROUGHOUT THE ENTIRE GALAXY!
THIS DESK IS EXTRAORDINARY... NO MATTER WHAT I DRAW...
IT SCANS AND ANIMATES A 3-D PROJECTION OF IT... IF ONLY I HAD ONE OF THESE ON EARTH... OR IN THE AFTERLIFE...
SQUARK!
HOW BORING OVER THERE...
BUT HERE...
THANKS TO YOU, MAYBE I'VE FINALLY FOUND THE PLACE...
WHERE I'LL FOREVER BE THE KING!
Welcome to PLANET KIRBY

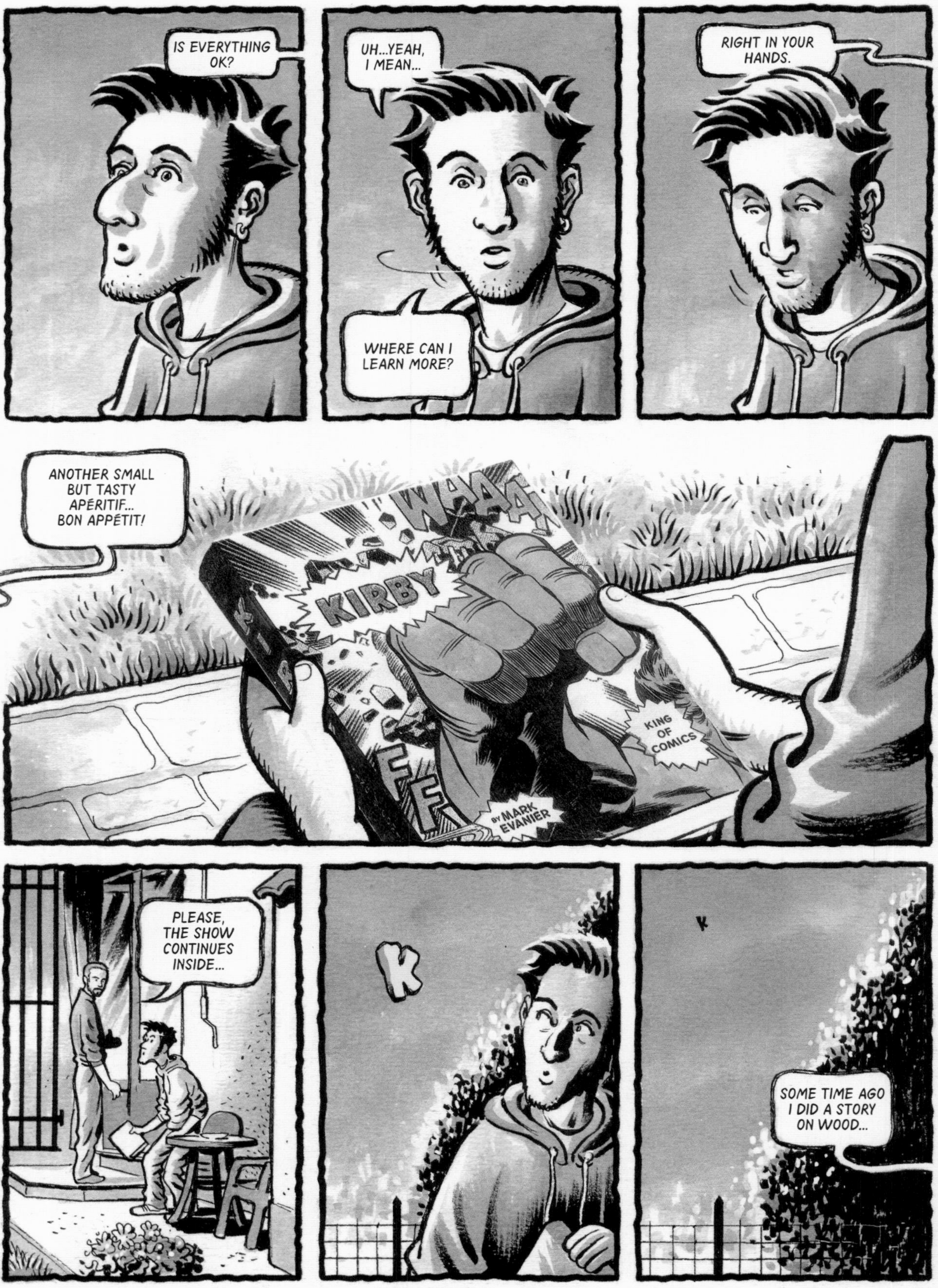
IS EVERYTHING OK?
UH...YEAH, I MEAN...
WHERE CAN I LEARN MORE?
RIGHT IN YOUR HANDS.
ANOTHER SMALL BUT TASTY APÉRITIF... BON APPÉTIT!
KIRBY
KING OF COMICS
BY MARK EVANIER
PLEASE, THE SHOW CONTINUES INSIDE...
K
SOME TIME AGO I DID A STORY ON WOOD...

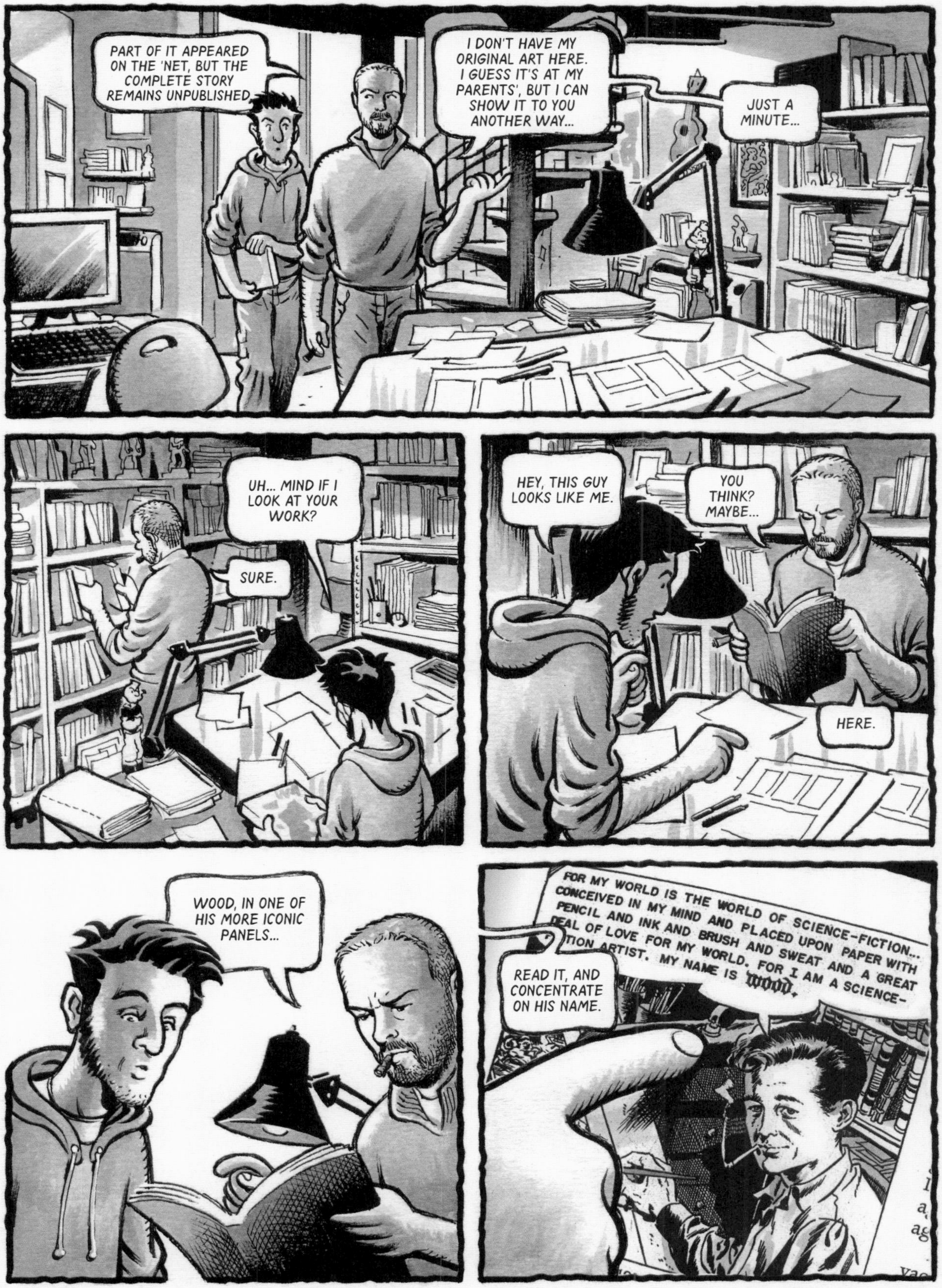
PART OF IT APPEARED ON THE 'NET, BUT THE COMPLETE STORY REMAINS UNPUBLISHED.
I DON'T HAVE MY ORIGINAL ART HERE. I GUESS IT'S AT MY PARENTS', BUT I CAN SHOW IT TO YOU ANOTHER WAY...
JUST A MINUTE...
UH... MIND IF I LOOK AT YOUR WORK?
SURE.
HEY, THIS GUY LOOKS LIKE ME.
YOU THINK? MAYBE...
HERE.
WOOD, IN ONE OF HIS MORE ICONIC PANELS...
FOR MY WORLD IS THE WORLD OF SCIENCE-FICTION... CONCEIVED IN MY MIND AND PLACED UPON PAPER WITH PENCIL AND INK AND BRUSH AND SWEAT AND A GREAT DEAL OF LOVE FOR MY WORLD. FOR I AM A SCIENCE-FICTION ARTIST. MY NAME IS WOOD.
READ IT, AND CONCENTRATE ON HIS NAME.

YOU'LL SEE IT CHANGE...

...ILD UPO... ...USH AND SWEAT WORLD. FOR I AM ...ME IS **wood.**

TAKE A CAREFUL LOOK AT THE LETTER "W"...

...D. FOR ...S **wood**

FOCUS... LIKE THAT...

...AND REVEAL WHAT'S INSIDE!

WOOD & me

Sergio Ponchione

Wally Wood was a gold coin, shining in the dark: dazzlingly bright, but with an ever-looming darkness underneath.

He was everything a cartoonist should and shouldn't be. An enormous, cursed talent. A tormented union of passion and pain. His dedication to his craft, combined with his love for the bottle, put his health at risk. If it's true that what you love destroys you, Wood is a shining example. I dislike excess, but I do share one of his temptations: work. If you do what you love, your job is your worst bad habit. Satisfaction results in addiction. Time spent not working feels wasted. When you work hard, you reach an altered state: an estrangement from the outside world and reality in general.

Wood in 1968

ALL ORGANIC MATERIAL IN ITS PATH.
TOM OR DICK OR HARRY WHILE I LISTEN TO
CURDLING SCREAMS ON MY INTERCOM...
THE MEN WHO

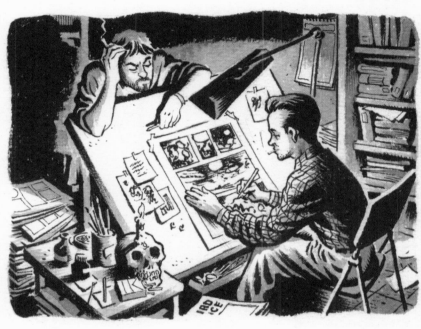

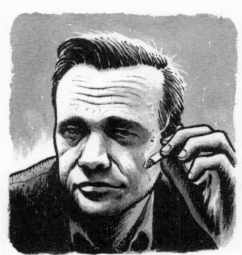

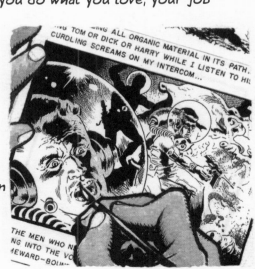

At work on "My World" (1953)

A perceptive anesthesia. A floating absence. Creating is an action that devours itself. No matter what you do, you're eager to do more. That may exhilarate you like nothing else can, but may also leave you completely drained. The act of creating overwhelms the creation. I'm imagining Wood's life like that, constantly busy, in the chase of the most irresistible and exhausting illusion of all: to always be the best.

The desire to maintain the illusion is on full display among the trees and cottages peppering the backgrounds of the Ray Bradbury adaptation "Mars Is Heaven!" These backgrounds actively deceive the story's protagonists—a group of astronauts who shockingly discover long-lost loved ones amidst jarringly familiar landscapes on the red planet. But after the smiles of joy from these reclaimed memories disappear, a disturbing suspicion that things aren't exactly as they seem begins to grow. When they find out what these beings really look like, it's too late.

Wood gives shape and substance to the illusion in a sublime but meaningful way that accentuates Bradbury's tale. Every single detail in his panels helps make the unreal as real to us as it is in the protagonists' eyes. Unfortunately, it's a skill he wasn't able to preserve over the years, eventually becoming a faded

"Mars Is Heaven!" (1953)

memory, leading to a fate more tragic than any EC twist ending.

But those days were still far away in 1953. Before that, he found much of the success he craved. A dream he had as a child, where he found a magic pencil that allowed him to draw like Alex Raymond, was more prescient than he could know.

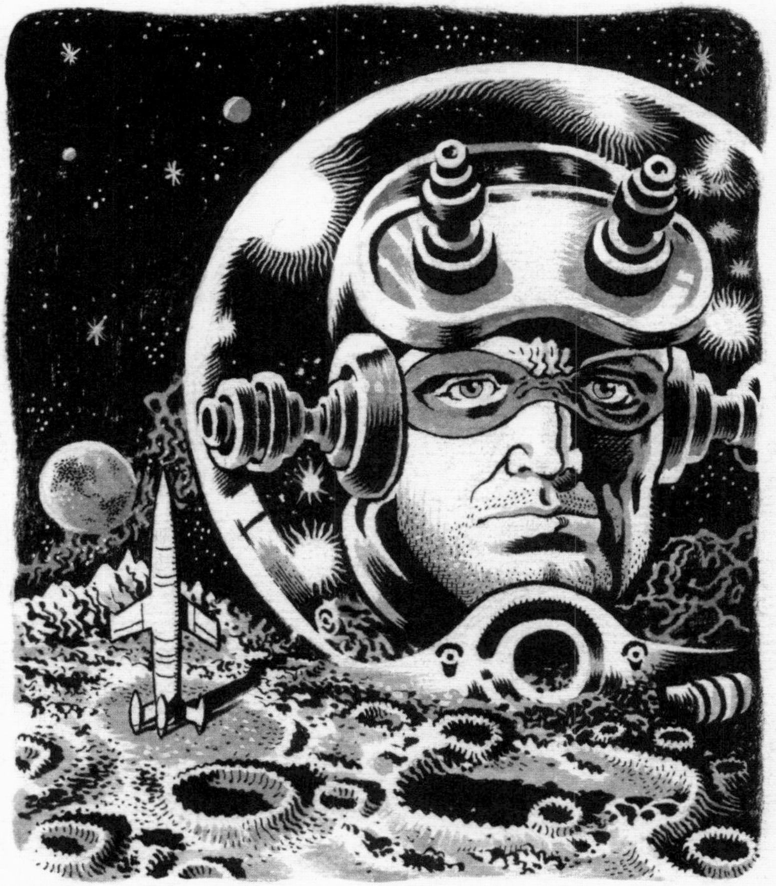

Wood pursued incredible dreams among the faraway stars and planets that he drew.

His drawings for *The Spirit*'s "Moon Saga" are masterful, black-and-white mosaics. Lights chase shadows over Zip-A-Tone-sodden ground, crawl over stones, lightning bolts; reflections slide over pipes and valves, bounce off between panels: most precious chiaroscuros that teach and tell more than a thousand captions.

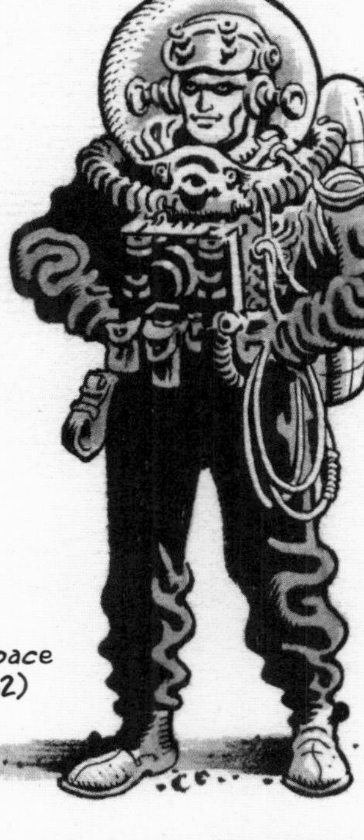

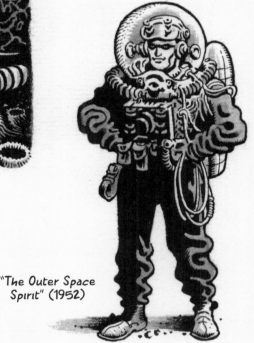

"The Outer Space Spirit" (1952)

No one had ever drawn space like that before. Many tried to do it after him. His evocative and unique craters, half-soaked in black, symbolize his art and reflect his life—the looming darkness would encompass the gold coin.

Among the stars, "Woody" shone with so much grace, yet on Earth he burned himself out with impossible hours hunched over his drawing table, day after day, night after night. Mountains of cigarettes, coffee, tea, and alcohol were his inevitable partners in this all-consuming lifestyle.

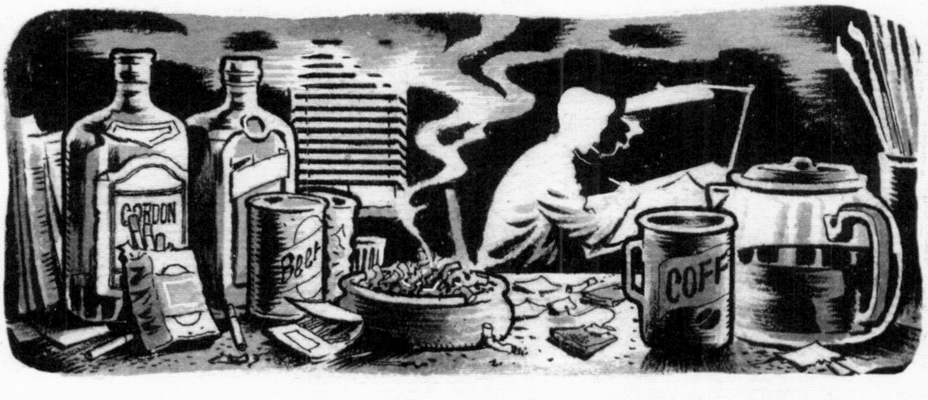
GORDON
Beer
COFF

Wood challenged himself, dueling with his own resistance. "There is only one Wally Wood, and that's me!," he posted on his studio wall.

The melancholy light in his eyes reveals a difficult and self-destructive personality. He was an unhappy guy and the work, once born from simple passion, became an exasperated form of therapy.

In his unforgettable *Mad* stories, the evocative irony of his style ruled. Footsteps echo through the fog in a perfect panel, and the comforting parody of so many dear old horror films touches me.

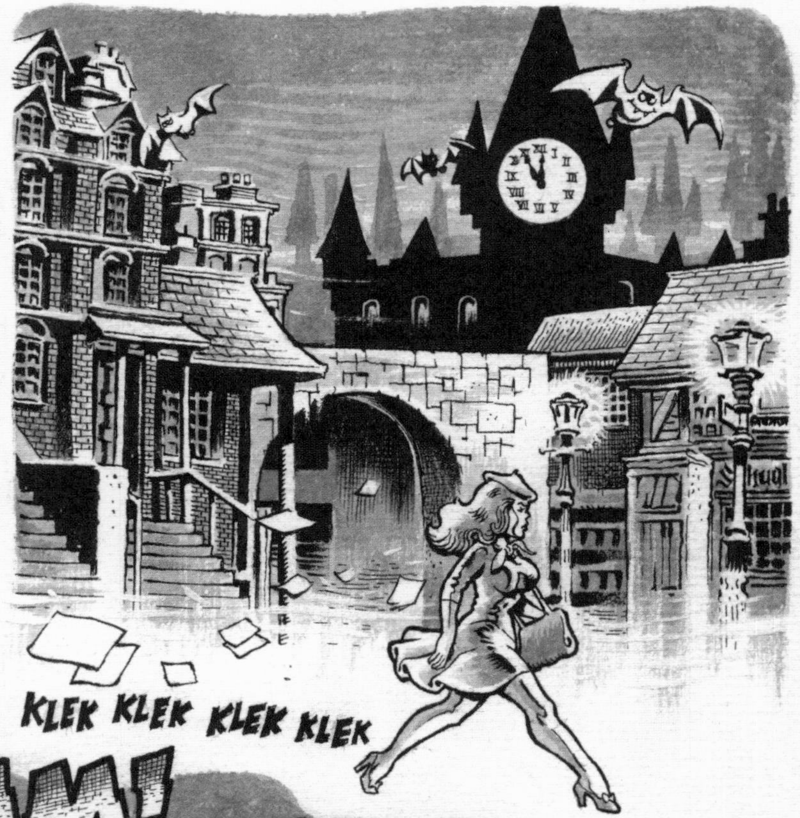
KLEK KLEK KLEK KLEK

"V-Vampires!" (1953)

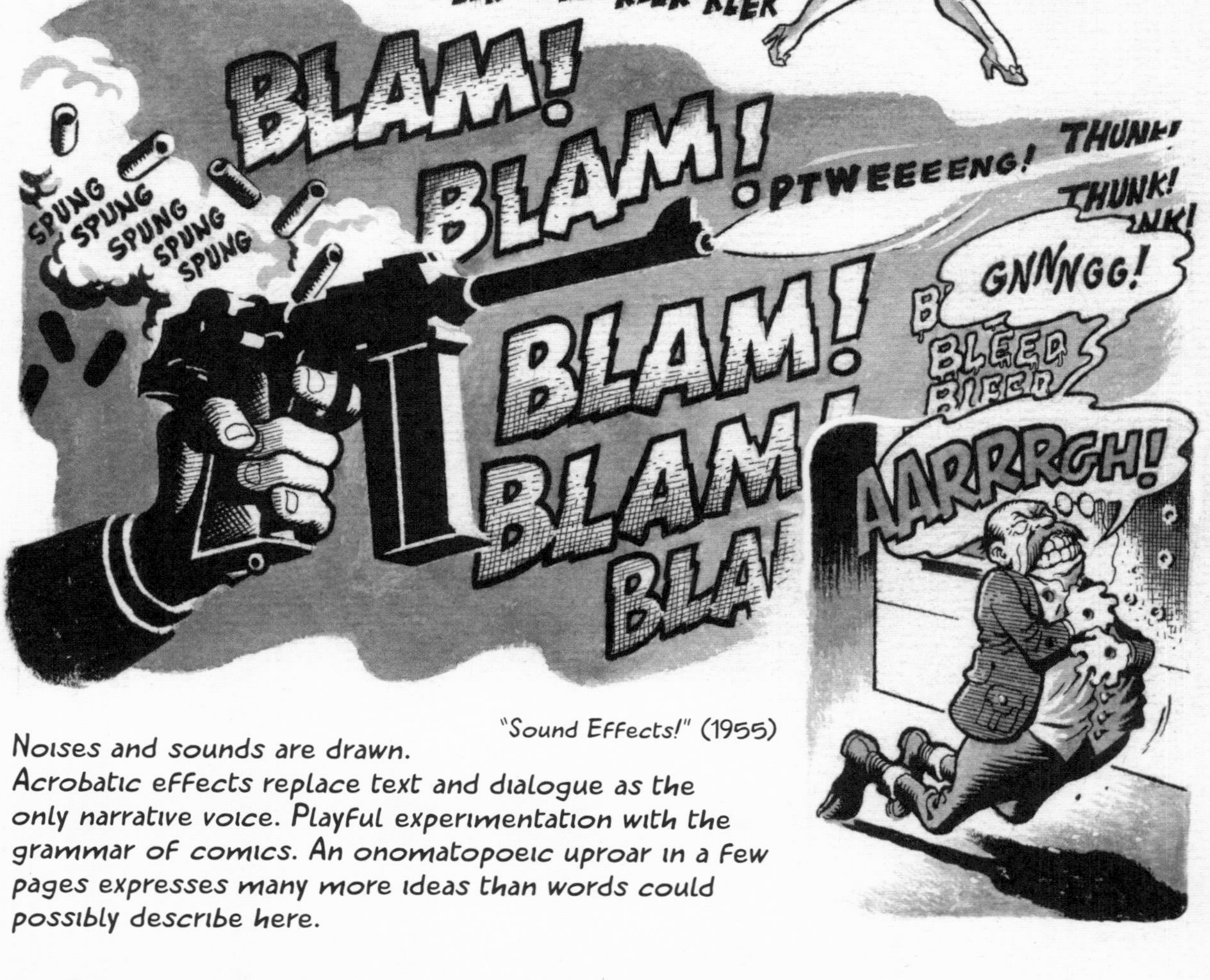
BLAM!
BLAM!
OPTWEEEENG!
THUNK!
SPUNG
SPUNG
SPUNG
SPUNG
SPUNG
GNNNGG!
BLAM!
BLAM!
BLEED
AARRRGH!

"Sound Effects!" (1955)

Noises and sounds are drawn.
Acrobatic effects replace text and dialogue as the only narrative voice. Playful experimentation with the grammar of comics. An onomatopoeic uproar in a few pages expresses many more ideas than words could possibly describe here.

Over the years, his face prematurely filled up with wrinkles, much like the ink-stained illustration boards on his table. Torment and excess undermined his mental and physical health, sending him into a downward spiral. Any illusions of grandeur became faded and distant. Worn away, depressed, and betrayed by his kidneys, he stared down the prospect of dialysis, and blinked.

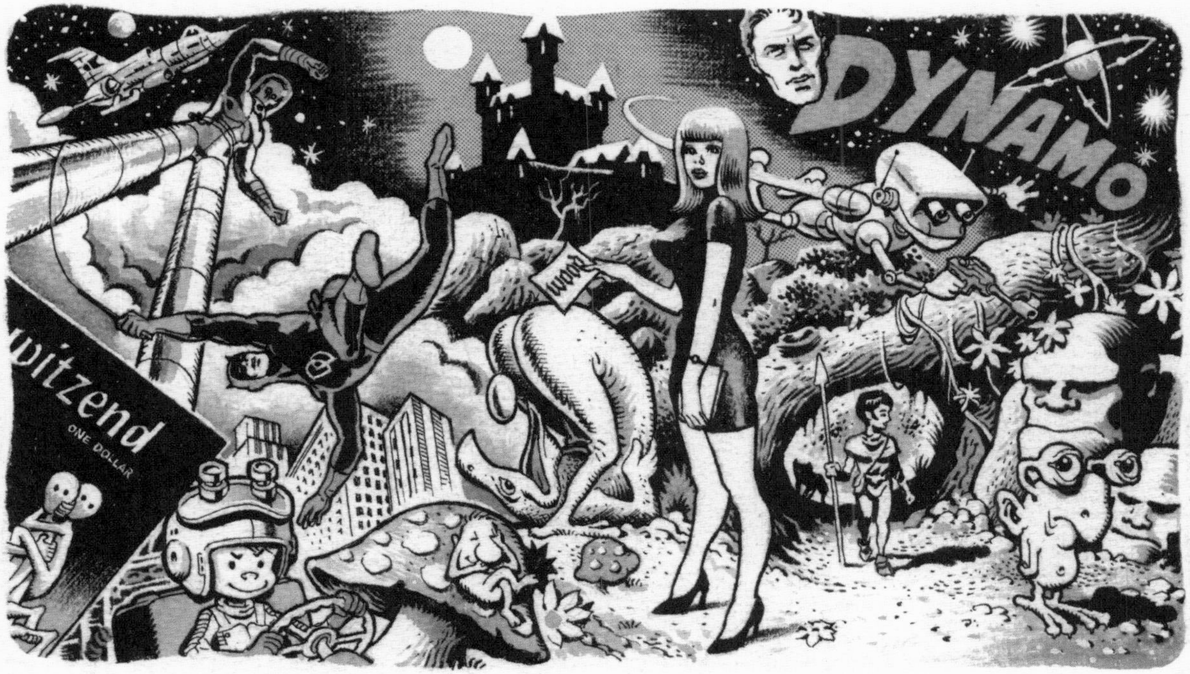
DYNAMO
wood
witzend
ONE DOLLAR

Wally Wood shot himself during the night of November 1, 1981, in his home near Hollywood. At the same time, at the New York Palladium, Frank Zappa performed his famous double Halloween concert, broadcast live on MTV. On the most sinister night of the year, specters and ghouls played maliciously with two of my favorite heroes: dragging one of them into eternal darkness and defiantly singing and dancing with the other.

On the other side of the world, unaware of all that, I slept in my six-and-a-half-year-old peaceful innocence, dreaming of who knows what.

Probably not of a magic pencil—but rather a gold coin, shining in the dark.

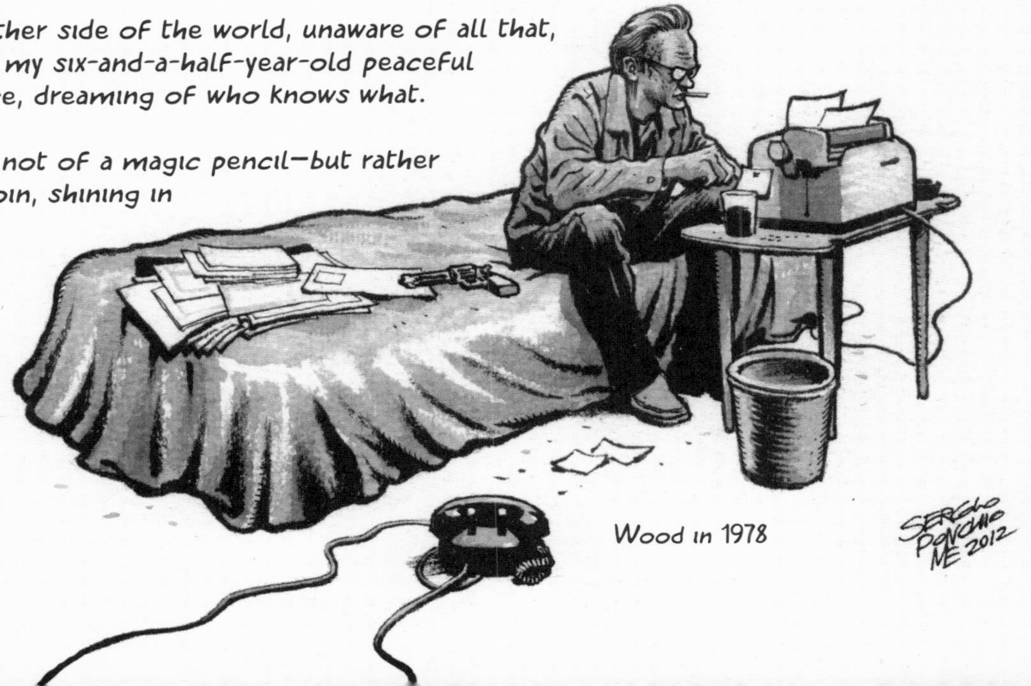
SERGIO PONCHIONE 2012

Wood in 1978

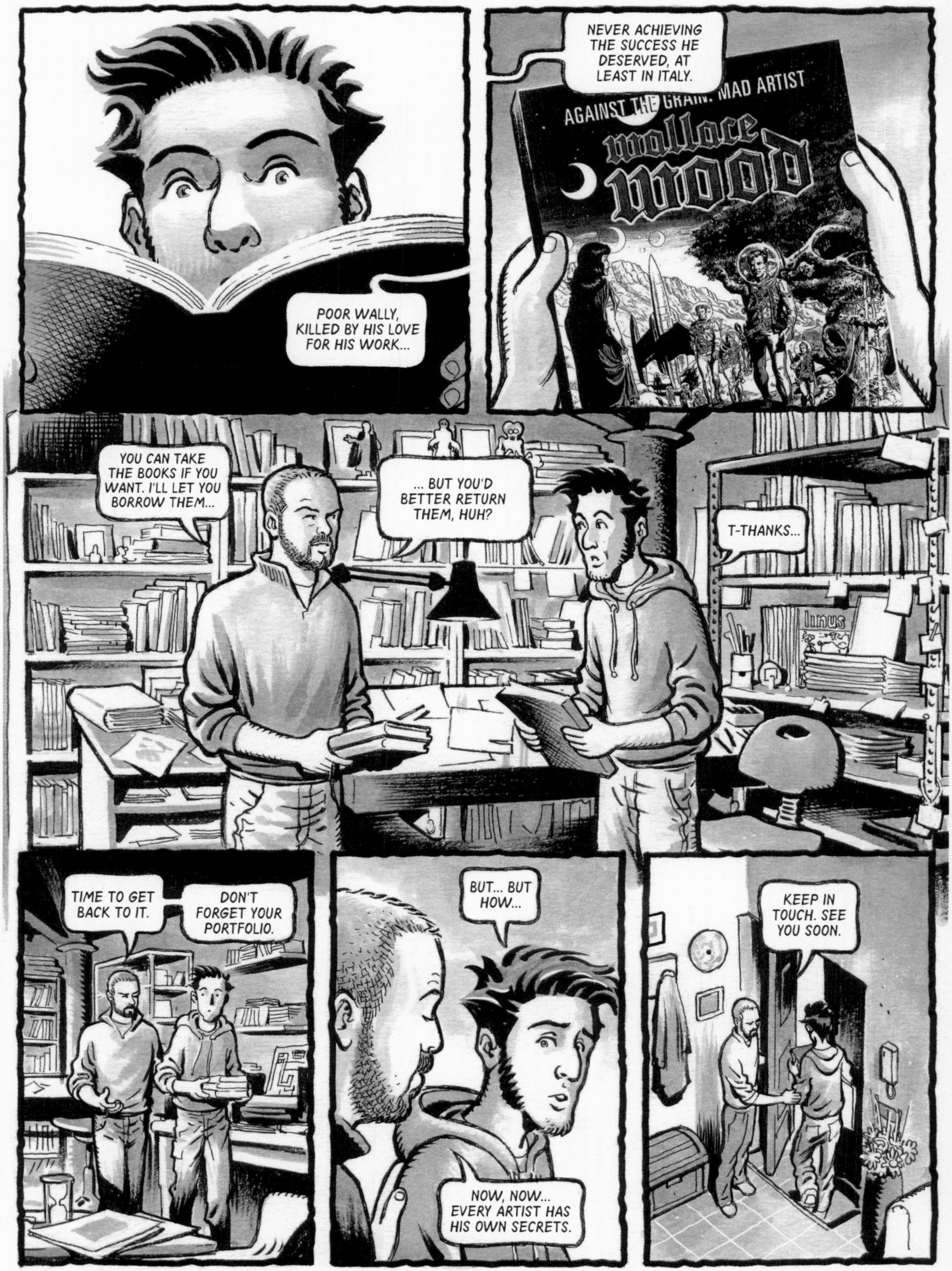
POOR WALLY, KILLED BY HIS LOVE FOR HIS WORK...
NEVER ACHIEVING THE SUCCESS HE DESERVED, AT LEAST IN ITALY.
AGAINST THE GRAIN: MAD ARTIST
wallace WOOD
YOU CAN TAKE THE BOOKS IF YOU WANT. I'LL LET YOU BORROW THEM...
... BUT YOU'D BETTER RETURN THEM, HUH?
T-THANKS...
linus
TIME TO GET BACK TO IT.
DON'T FORGET YOUR PORTFOLIO.
BUT... BUT HOW...
NOW, NOW... EVERY ARTIST HAS HIS OWN SECRETS.
KEEP IN TOUCH. SEE YOU SOON.

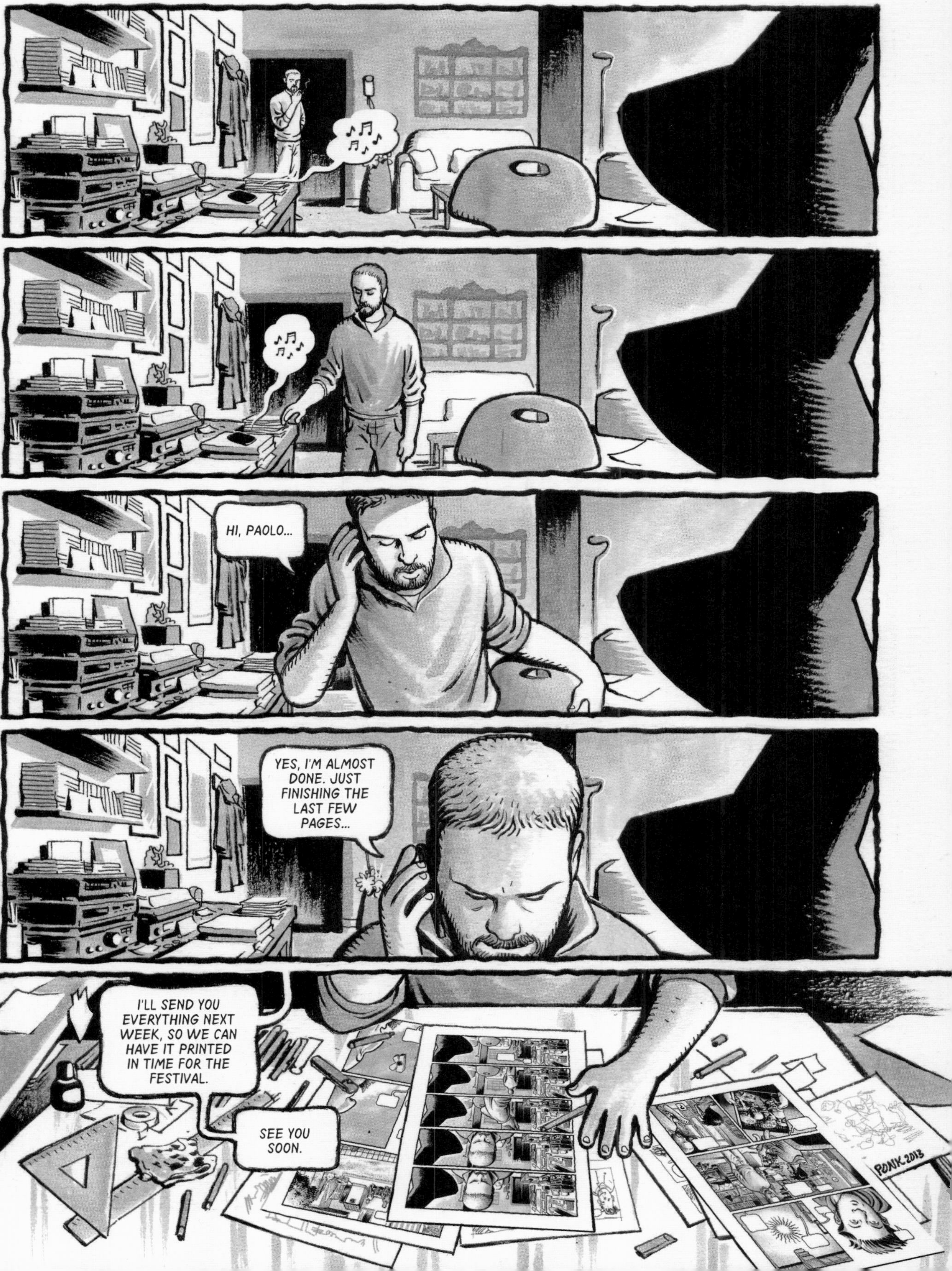
HI, PAOLO...
YES, I'M ALMOST DONE. JUST FINISHING THE LAST FEW PAGES...
I'LL SEND YOU EVERYTHING NEXT WEEK, SO WE CAN HAVE IT PRINTED IN TIME FOR THE FESTIVAL.
SEE YOU SOON.
PONK 2013

2017. FOUR YEARS LATER.

... SO I DECIDED TO KEEP DOING SHORT STORIES ABOUT CARTOONISTS, TO COLLECT AS A BOOK.

THE TITLE IS *MEMORABILIA,* FOR NOW.

IGORT SUGGESTED IT.

I KIND OF LIKE IT, ALTHOUGH IT'S A BIT NOSTALGIC. WE'LL SEE.

I'D LIKE TO DO STORIES ABOUT EISNER, TOTH, SEGAR, CRUMB, AND OTHERS. EVERYONE CONNECTED TO MY EVERYDAY LIFE.

I'LL TELL YOU MORE LATER.

TAKE CARE OF YOURSELF, PAOLO. BYE.

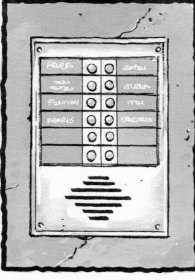

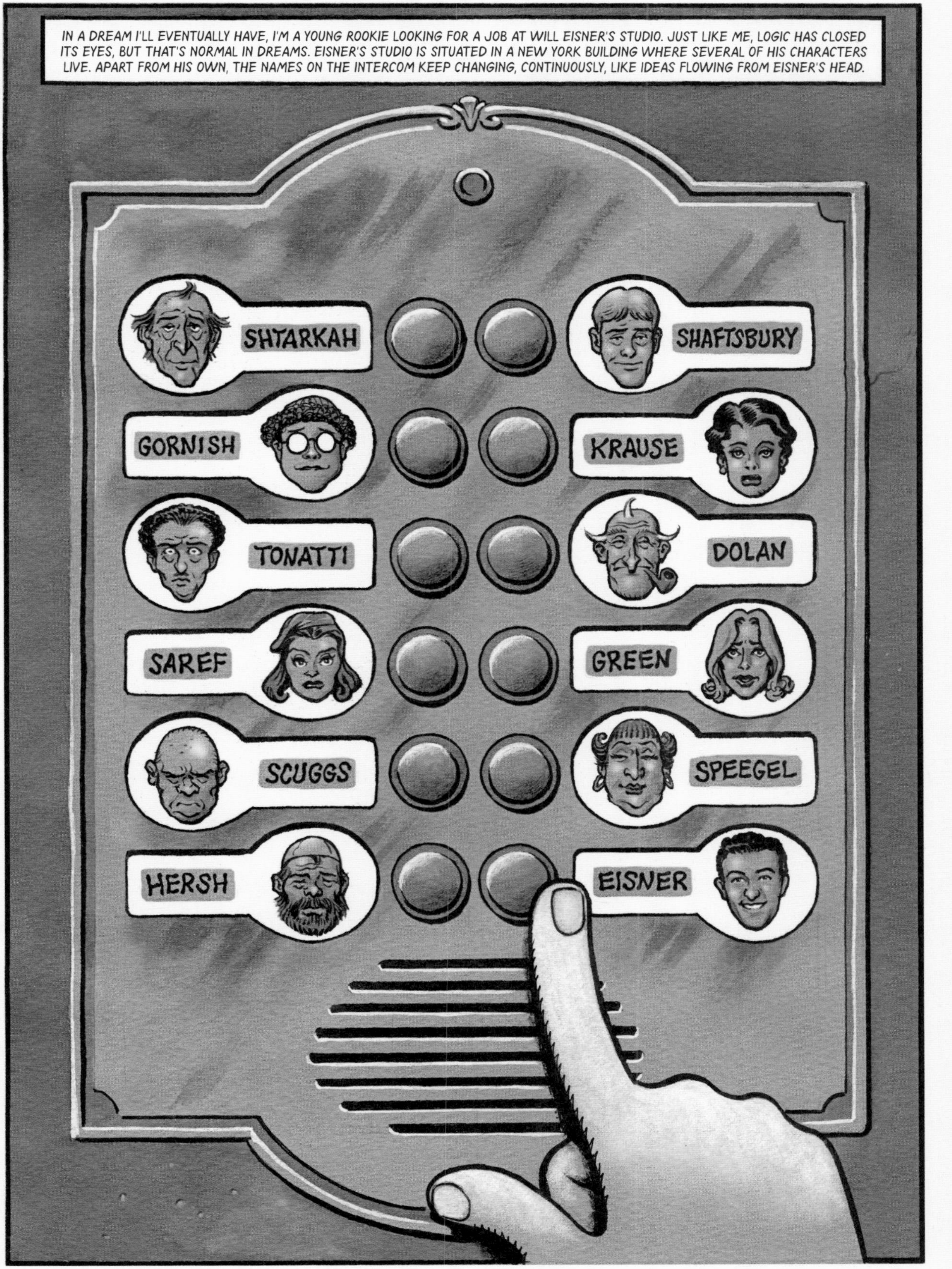
IN A DREAM I'LL EVENTUALLY HAVE, I'M A YOUNG ROOKIE LOOKING FOR A JOB AT WILL EISNER'S STUDIO. JUST LIKE ME, LOGIC HAS CLOSED ITS EYES, BUT THAT'S NORMAL IN DREAMS. EISNER'S STUDIO IS SITUATED IN A NEW YORK BUILDING WHERE SEVERAL OF HIS CHARACTERS LIVE. APART FROM HIS OWN, THE NAMES ON THE INTERCOM KEEP CHANGING, CONTINUOUSLY, LIKE IDEAS FLOWING FROM EISNER'S HEAD.
SHTARKAH
SHAFTSBURY
GORNISH
KRAUSE
TONATTI
DOLAN
SAREF
GREEN
SCUGGS
SPEEGEL
HERSH
EISNER

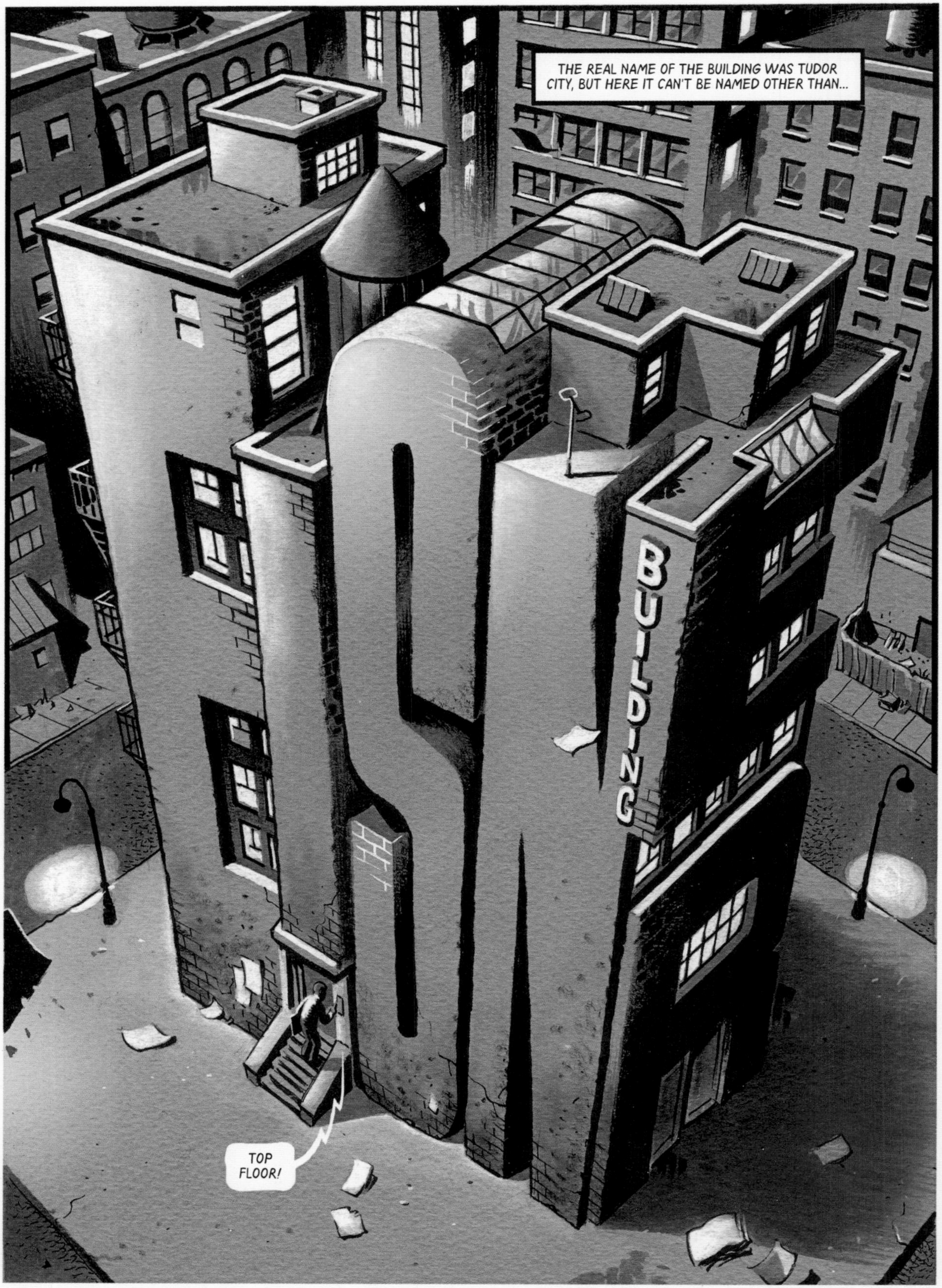
THE REAL NAME OF THE BUILDING WAS TUDOR CITY, BUT HERE IT CAN'T BE NAMED OTHER THAN...
BUILDING
TOP FLOOR!

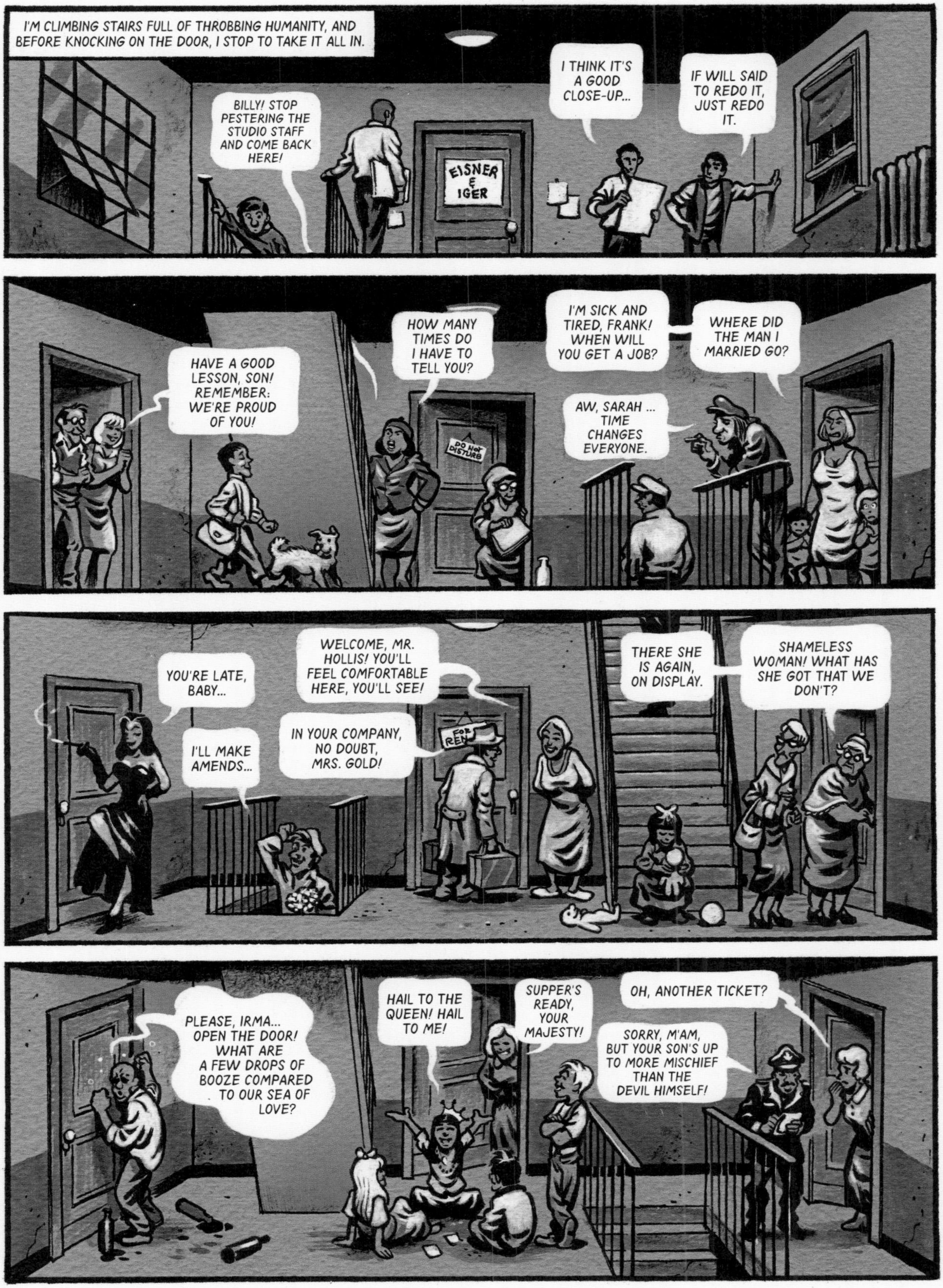

I'M CLIMBING STAIRS FULL OF THROBBING HUMANITY, AND BEFORE KNOCKING ON THE DOOR, I STOP TO TAKE IT ALL IN.
BILLY! STOP PESTERING THE STUDIO STAFF AND COME BACK HERE!
EISNER & IGER
I THINK IT'S A GOOD CLOSE-UP...
IF WILL SAID TO REDO IT, JUST REDO IT.
HAVE A GOOD LESSON, SON! REMEMBER: WE'RE PROUD OF YOU!
HOW MANY TIMES DO I HAVE TO TELL YOU?
DO NOT DISTURB
I'M SICK AND TIRED, FRANK! WHEN WILL YOU GET A JOB?
WHERE DID THE MAN I MARRIED GO?
AW, SARAH ... TIME CHANGES EVERYONE.
YOU'RE LATE, BABY...
I'LL MAKE AMENDS...
WELCOME, MR. HOLLIS! YOU'LL FEEL COMFORTABLE HERE, YOU'LL SEE!
IN YOUR COMPANY, NO DOUBT, MRS. GOLD!
FOR RENT
THERE SHE IS AGAIN, ON DISPLAY.
SHAMELESS WOMAN! WHAT HAS SHE GOT THAT WE DON'T?
PLEASE, IRMA... OPEN THE DOOR! WHAT ARE A FEW DROPS OF BOOZE COMPARED TO OUR SEA OF LOVE?
HAIL TO THE QUEEN! HAIL TO ME!
SUPPER'S READY, YOUR MAJESTY!
OH, ANOTHER TICKET?
SORRY, M'AM, BUT YOUR SON'S UP TO MORE MISCHIEF THAN THE DEVIL HIMSELF!

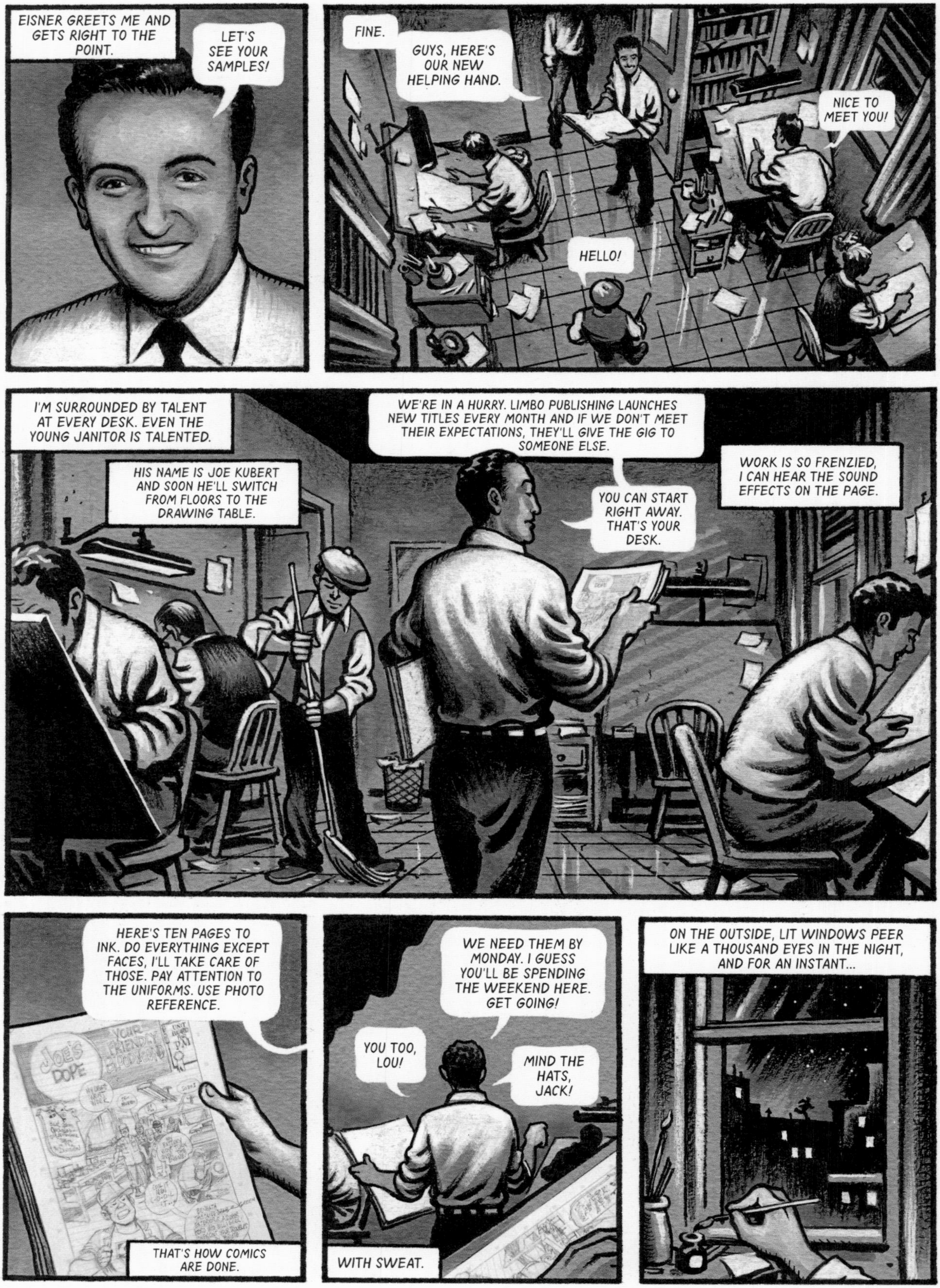
EISNER GREETS ME AND GETS RIGHT TO THE POINT.
LET'S SEE YOUR SAMPLES!
FINE.
GUYS, HERE'S OUR NEW HELPING HAND.
NICE TO MEET YOU!
HELLO!
I'M SURROUNDED BY TALENT AT EVERY DESK. EVEN THE YOUNG JANITOR IS TALENTED.
HIS NAME IS JOE KUBERT AND SOON HE'LL SWITCH FROM FLOORS TO THE DRAWING TABLE.
WE'RE IN A HURRY. LIMBO PUBLISHING LAUNCHES NEW TITLES EVERY MONTH AND IF WE DON'T MEET THEIR EXPECTATIONS, THEY'LL GIVE THE GIG TO SOMEONE ELSE.
YOU CAN START RIGHT AWAY. THAT'S YOUR DESK.
WORK IS SO FRENZIED, I CAN HEAR THE SOUND EFFECTS ON THE PAGE.
HERE'S TEN PAGES TO INK. DO EVERYTHING EXCEPT FACES, I'LL TAKE CARE OF THOSE. PAY ATTENTION TO THE UNIFORMS. USE PHOTO REFERENCE.
JOE'S DOPE
YOUR FRIENDLY BROTHER
THAT'S HOW COMICS ARE DONE.
WE NEED THEM BY MONDAY. I GUESS YOU'LL BE SPENDING THE WEEKEND HERE. GET GOING!
YOU TOO, LOU!
MIND THE HATS, JACK!
WITH SWEAT.
ON THE OUTSIDE, LIT WINDOWS PEER LIKE A THOUSAND EYES IN THE NIGHT, AND FOR AN INSTANT...

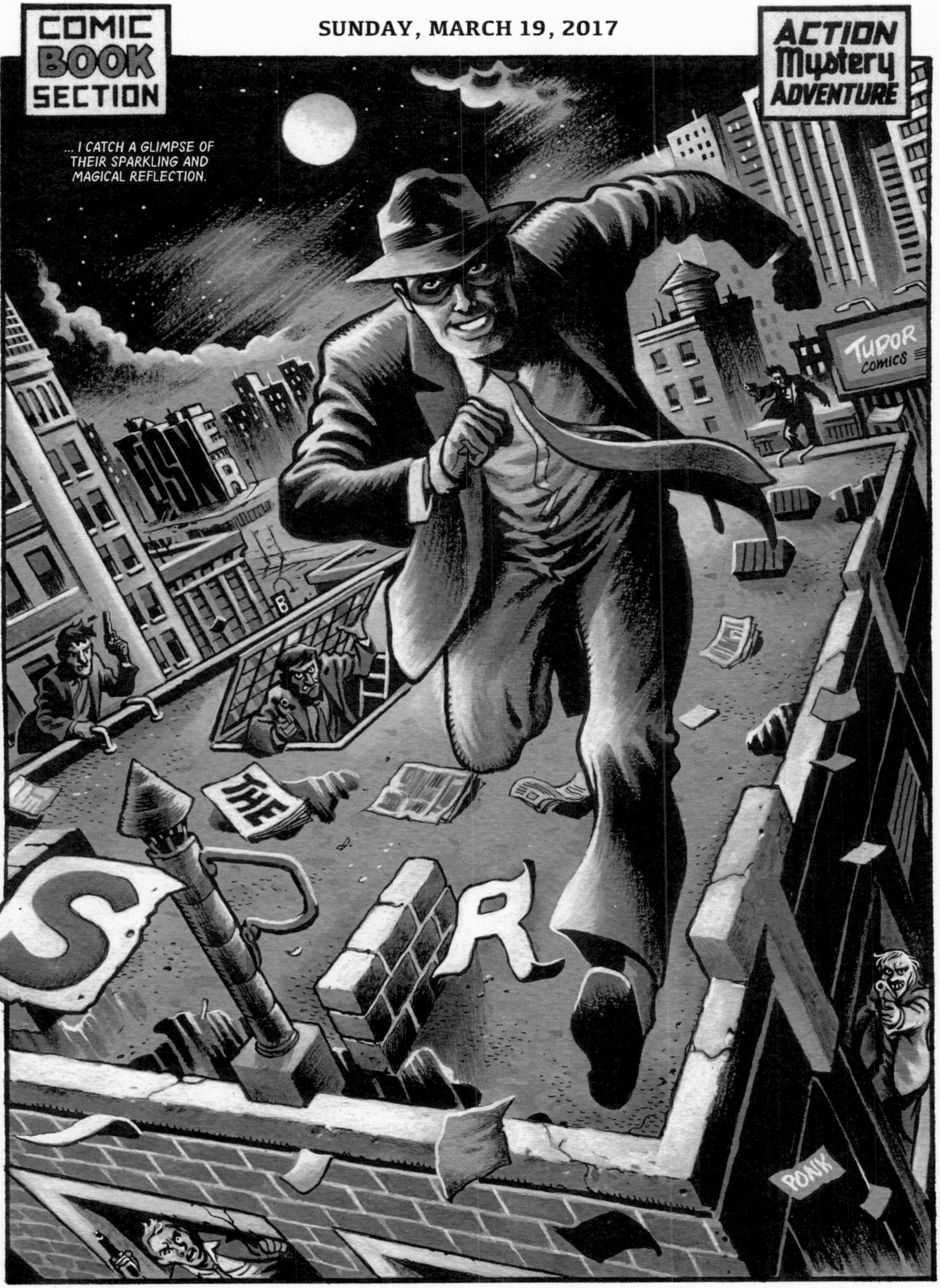
COMIC BOOK SECTION
SUNDAY, MARCH 19, 2017
ACTION Mystery ADVENTURE
... I CATCH A GLIMPSE OF THEIR SPARKLING AND MAGICAL REFLECTION.
TUDOR COMICS
THE
PONK

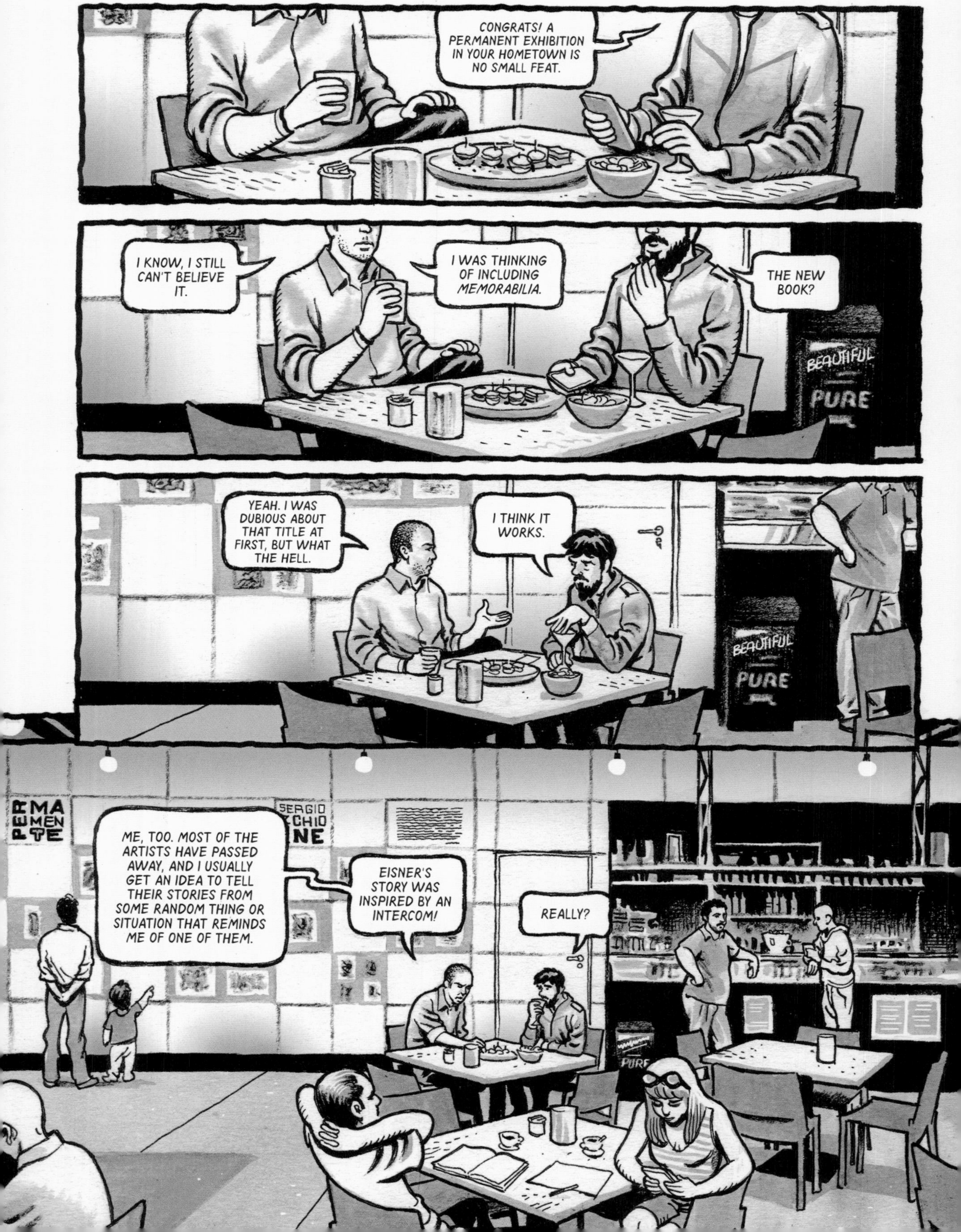
CONGRATS! A PERMANENT EXHIBITION IN YOUR HOMETOWN IS NO SMALL FEAT.
I KNOW, I STILL CAN'T BELIEVE IT.
I WAS THINKING OF INCLUDING MEMORABILIA.
THE NEW BOOK?
BEAUTIFUL
PURE
YEAH. I WAS DUBIOUS ABOUT THAT TITLE AT FIRST, BUT WHAT THE HELL.
I THINK IT WORKS.
BEAUTIFUL
PURE
PER MA NEN TE
SERGIO ZCHIO NE
ME, TOO. MOST OF THE ARTISTS HAVE PASSED AWAY, AND I USUALLY GET AN IDEA TO TELL THEIR STORIES FROM SOME RANDOM THING OR SITUATION THAT REMINDS ME OF ONE OF THEM.
EISNER'S STORY WAS INSPIRED BY AN INTERCOM!
REALLY?

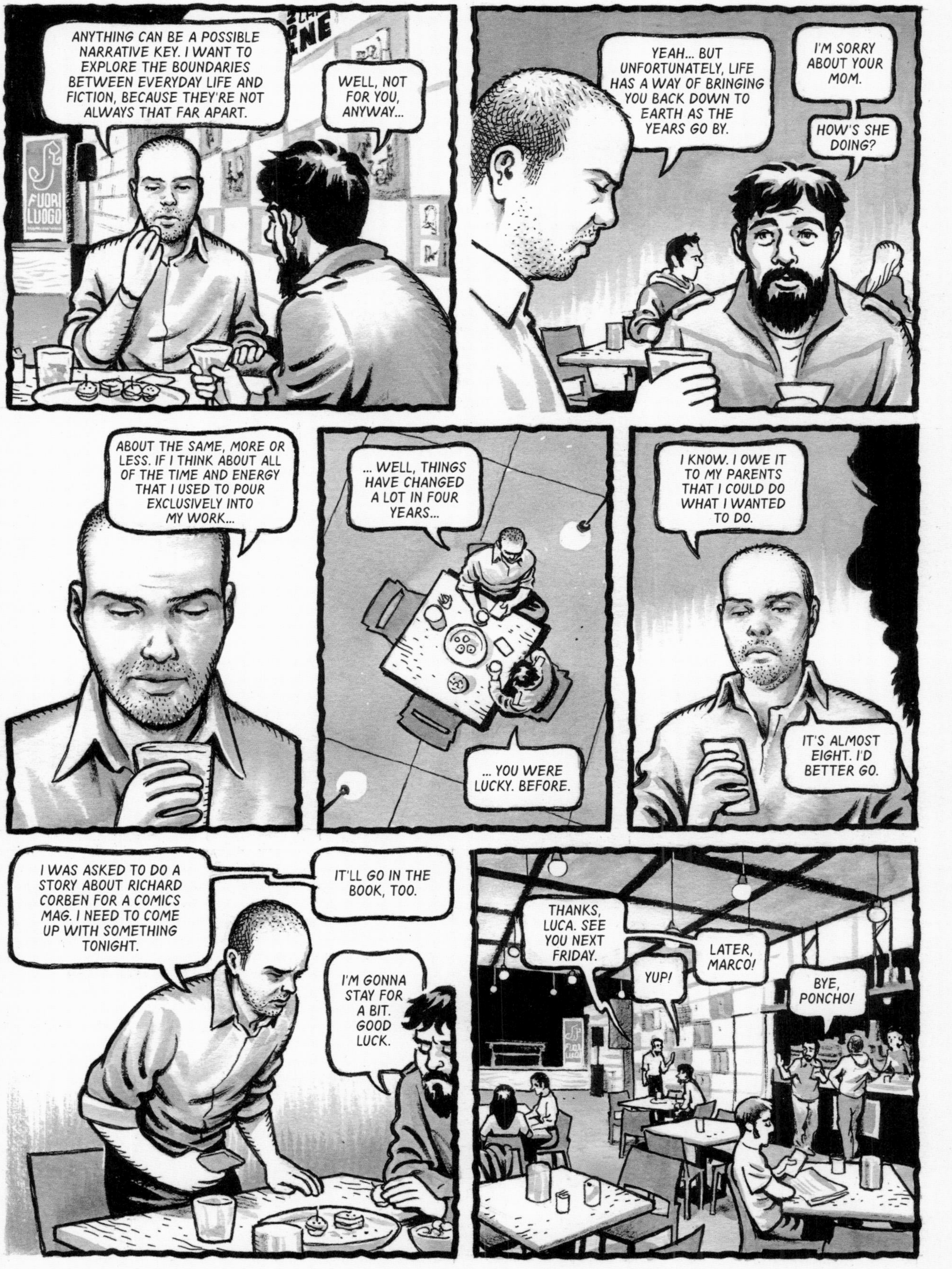

ANYTHING CAN BE A POSSIBLE NARRATIVE KEY. I WANT TO EXPLORE THE BOUNDARIES BETWEEN EVERYDAY LIFE AND FICTION, BECAUSE THEY'RE NOT ALWAYS THAT FAR APART.
WELL, NOT FOR YOU, ANYWAY...
FUORI LUOGO
YEAH... BUT UNFORTUNATELY, LIFE HAS A WAY OF BRINGING YOU BACK DOWN TO EARTH AS THE YEARS GO BY.
I'M SORRY ABOUT YOUR MOM.
HOW'S SHE DOING?
ABOUT THE SAME, MORE OR LESS. IF I THINK ABOUT ALL OF THE TIME AND ENERGY THAT I USED TO POUR EXCLUSIVELY INTO MY WORK...
... WELL, THINGS HAVE CHANGED A LOT IN FOUR YEARS...
... YOU WERE LUCKY. BEFORE.
I KNOW. I OWE IT TO MY PARENTS THAT I COULD DO WHAT I WANTED TO DO.
IT'S ALMOST EIGHT. I'D BETTER GO.
I WAS ASKED TO DO A STORY ABOUT RICHARD CORBEN FOR A COMICS MAG. I NEED TO COME UP WITH SOMETHING TONIGHT.
IT'LL GO IN THE BOOK, TOO.
I'M GONNA STAY FOR A BIT. GOOD LUCK.
THANKS, LUCA. SEE YOU NEXT FRIDAY.
YUP!
LATER, MARCO!
BYE, PONCHO!

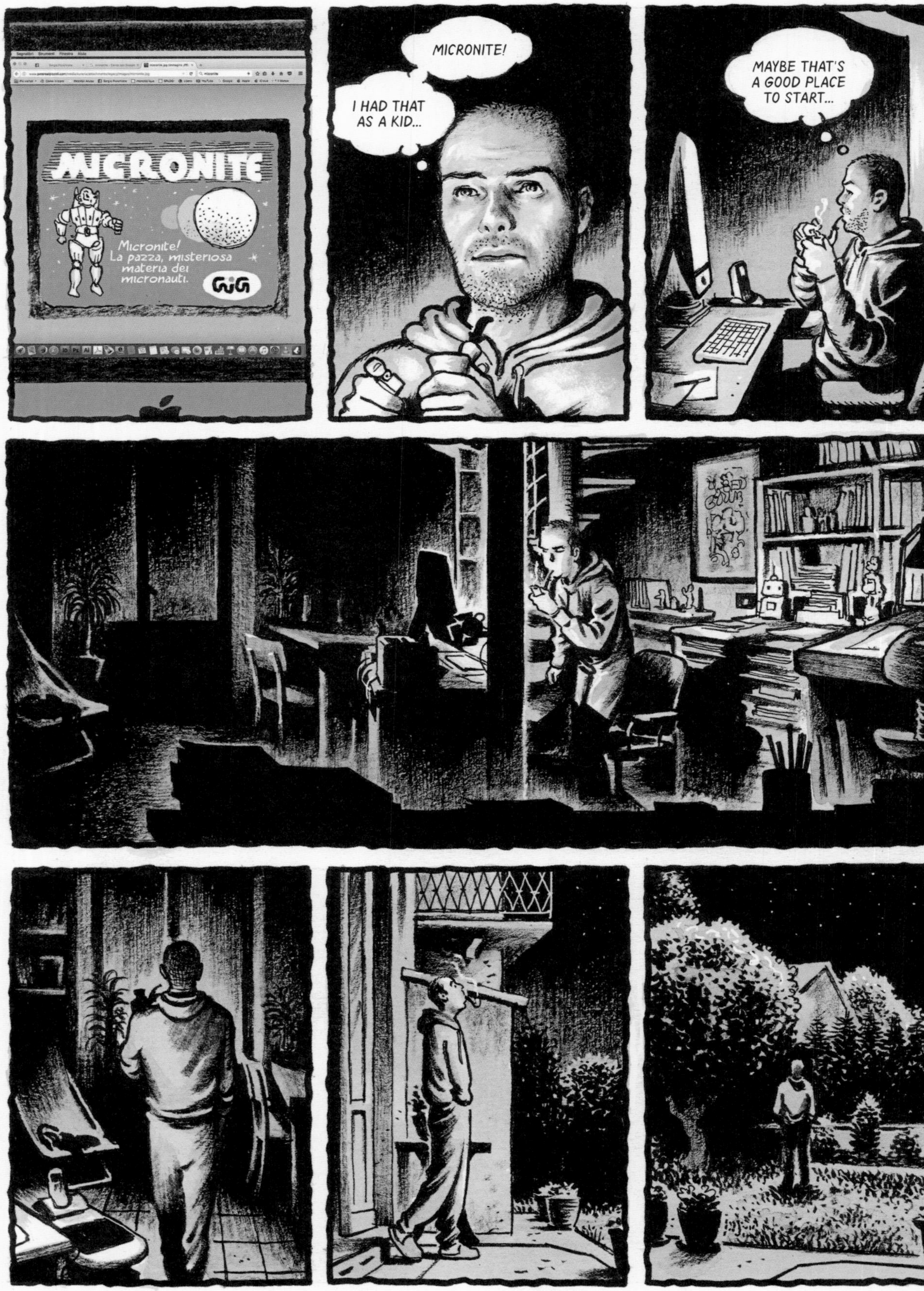

MICRONITE
Micronite!
La pazza, misteriosa
materia dei
micronauti.
MICRONITE!
I HAD THAT
AS A KID...
MAYBE THAT'S
A GOOD PLACE
TO START...

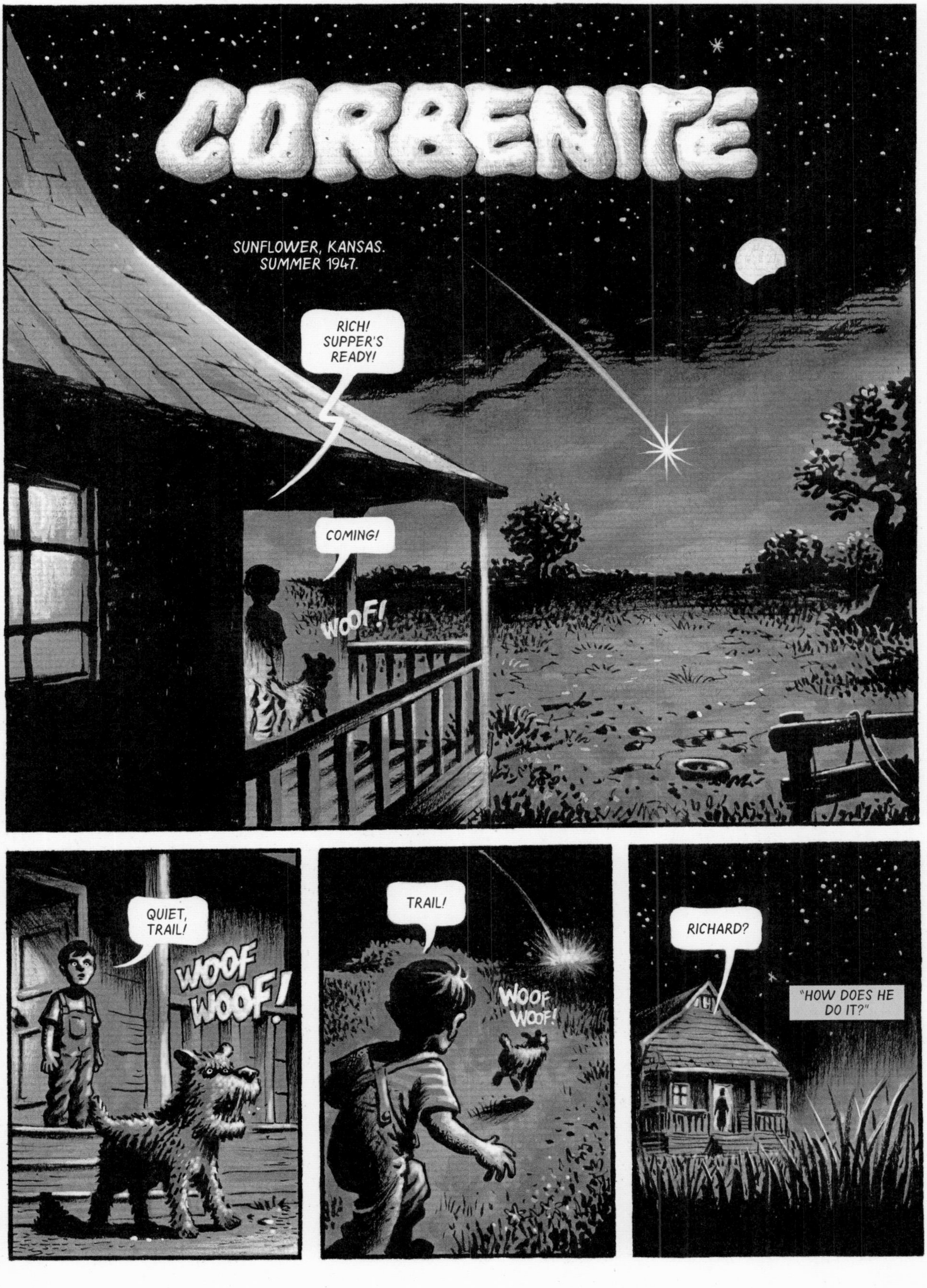
CORBENITE
SUNFLOWER, KANSAS. SUMMER 1947.
RICH! SUPPER'S READY!
COMING!
WOOF!
QUIET, TRAIL!
WOOF WOOF!
TRAIL!
WOOF WOOF!
RICHARD?
"HOW DOES HE DO IT?"

"IT'S ALL ABOUT SHAPES."

"IT'S MIND-BLOWING. DID YOU TALK TECHNIQUES?"

"SURE. PENCIL-SHADED INKS, FELT-TIP PENS, AIRBRUSH, AND THEN COMPUTERS, TOO. VERY PERSONAL AND PAINSTAKING COLORING."

WOOF WOOF!

"IT TAKES A LOT OF TIME AND ENERGY. AND YET HE MADE A LOT OF STUFF."

"YOU NEED MUSCLES TO MAKE COMICS."

"HE'S GOT THEM."

"YEAH?"

WOOF!

"BODY BUILDING."

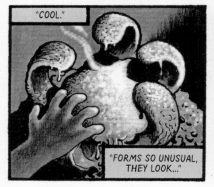

"COOL."

"FORMS SO UNUSUAL, THEY LOOK..."

"... LIKE THEY'RE FROM ANOTHER WORLD."

WOOF WOOF!

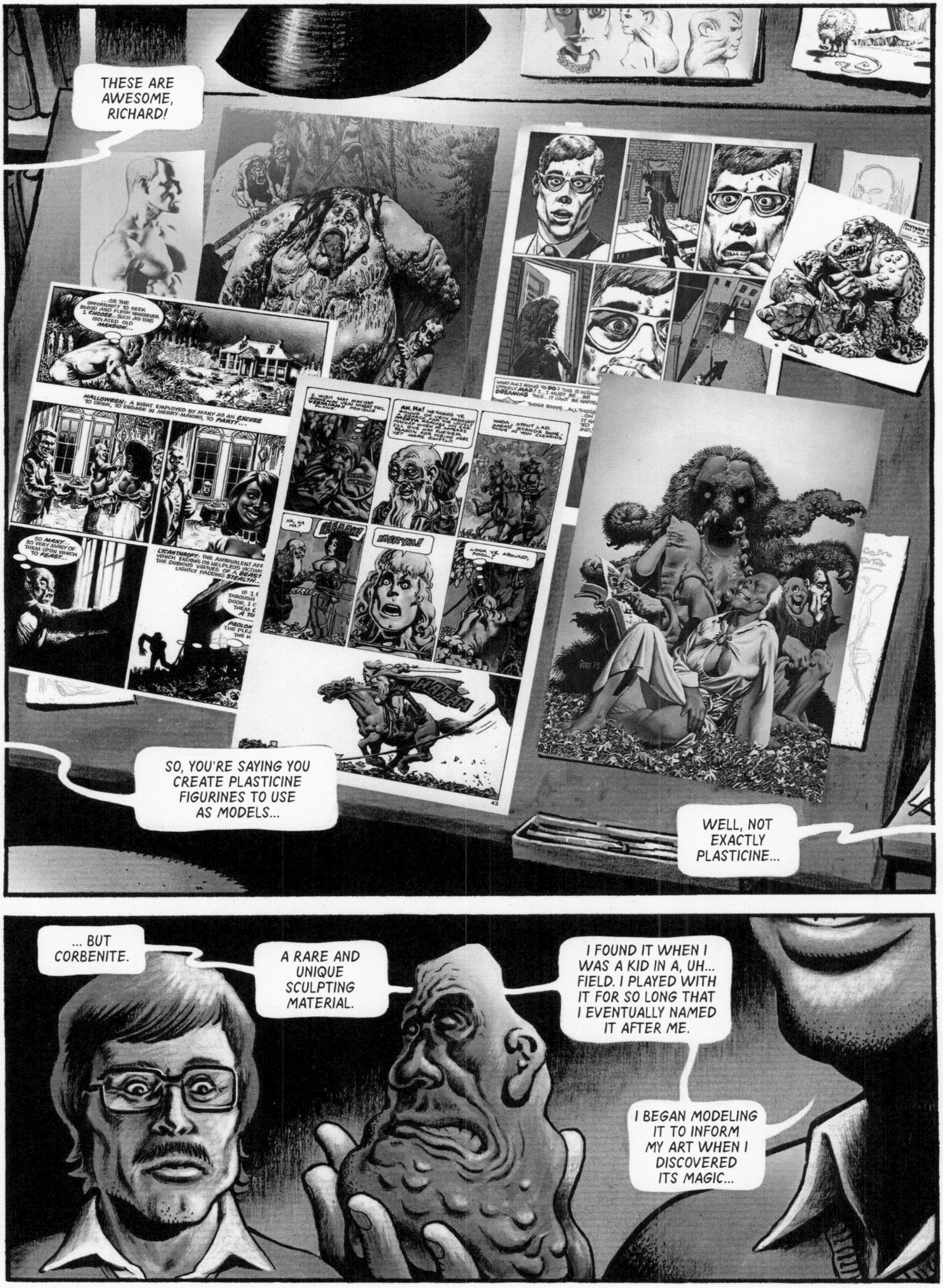

THESE ARE AWESOME, RICHARD!
SO, YOU'RE SAYING YOU CREATE PLASTICINE FIGURINES TO USE AS MODELS...
WELL, NOT EXACTLY PLASTICINE...
... BUT CORBENITE.
A RARE AND UNIQUE SCULPTING MATERIAL.
I FOUND IT WHEN I WAS A KID IN A, UH... FIELD. I PLAYED WITH IT FOR SO LONG THAT I EVENTUALLY NAMED IT AFTER ME.
I BEGAN MODELING IT TO INFORM MY ART WHEN I DISCOVERED ITS MAGIC...

IT HEIGHTENS MY VISUAL IMAGINATION... I CREATED CHARACTERS LIKE I NEVER HAD BEFORE...

SOMETIMES IT TAKES ON COLORS I'VE NEVER EVEN SEEN, WHICH I TRY TO REPRODUCE...

...RESTLESS AND INTENSE CHIAROSCUROS WRITHE WITHOUT ANY LIGHT.

WHEN I'M CREATING A CHARACTER, I HANDLE IT, I CONCENTRATE...

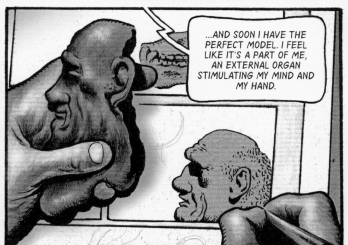

...AND SOON I HAVE THE PERFECT MODEL. I FEEL LIKE IT'S A PART OF ME, AN EXTERNAL ORGAN STIMULATING MY MIND AND MY HAND.

I THINK I WAS MEANT TO FIND IT...

"LISTEN HERE..."

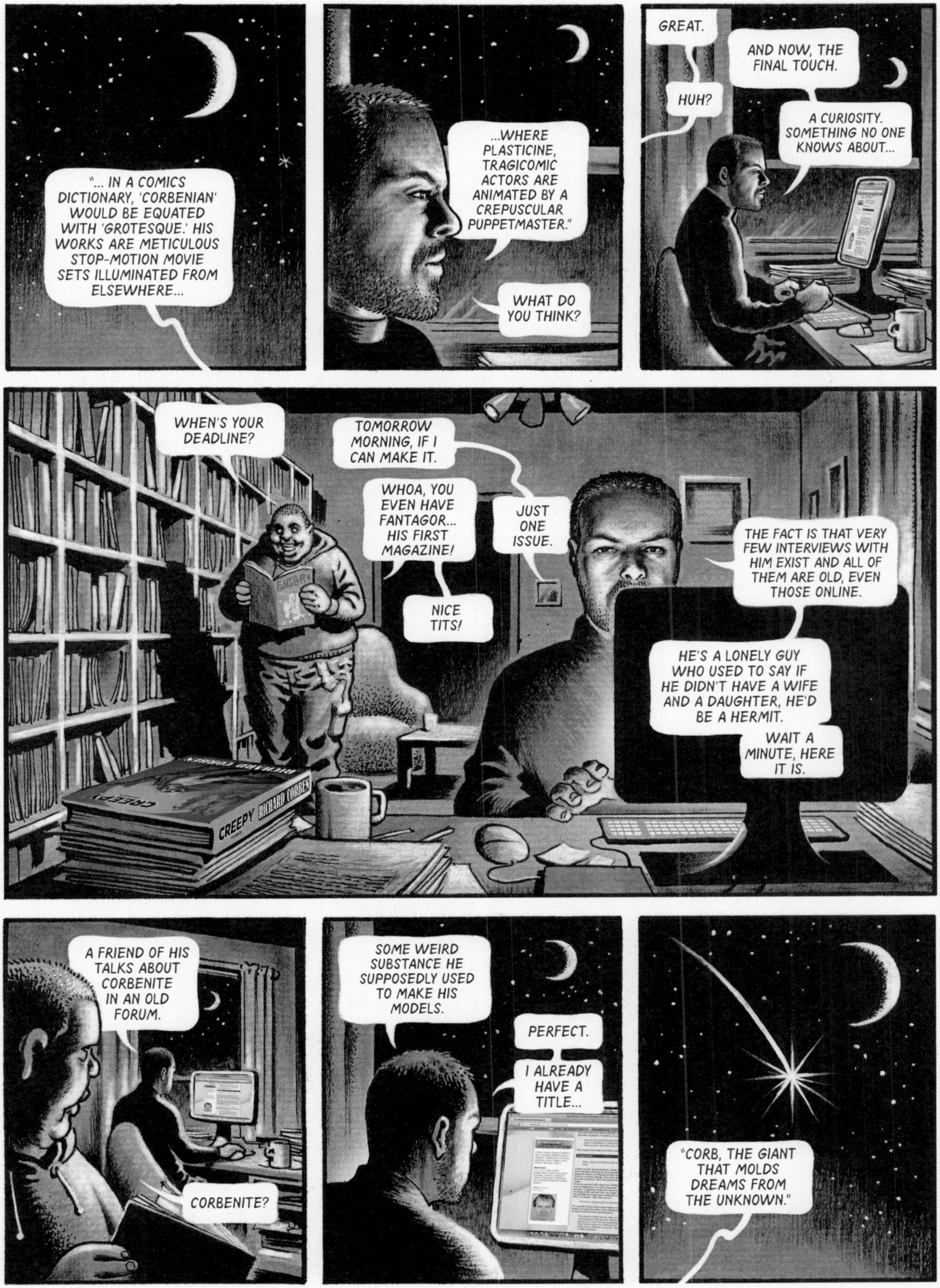
"... IN A COMICS DICTIONARY, 'CORBENIAN' WOULD BE EQUATED WITH 'GROTESQUE.' HIS WORKS ARE METICULOUS STOP-MOTION MOVIE SETS ILLUMINATED FROM ELSEWHERE...
...WHERE PLASTICINE, TRAGICOMIC ACTORS ARE ANIMATED BY A CREPUSCULAR PUPPETMASTER."
WHAT DO YOU THINK?
GREAT.
HUH?
AND NOW, THE FINAL TOUCH.
A CURIOSITY. SOMETHING NO ONE KNOWS ABOUT...
WHEN'S YOUR DEADLINE?
TOMORROW MORNING, IF I CAN MAKE IT.
WHOA, YOU EVEN HAVE FANTAGOR... HIS FIRST MAGAZINE!
JUST ONE ISSUE.
NICE TITS!
THE FACT IS THAT VERY FEW INTERVIEWS WITH HIM EXIST AND ALL OF THEM ARE OLD, EVEN THOSE ONLINE.
HE'S A LONELY GUY WHO USED TO SAY IF HE DIDN'T HAVE A WIFE AND A DAUGHTER, HE'D BE A HERMIT.
WAIT A MINUTE, HERE IT IS.
CREEPY RICHARD CORBEN
A FRIEND OF HIS TALKS ABOUT CORBENITE IN AN OLD FORUM.
CORBENITE?
SOME WEIRD SUBSTANCE HE SUPPOSEDLY USED TO MAKE HIS MODELS.
PERFECT.
I ALREADY HAVE A TITLE...
"CORB, THE GIANT THAT MOLDS DREAMS FROM THE UNKNOWN."

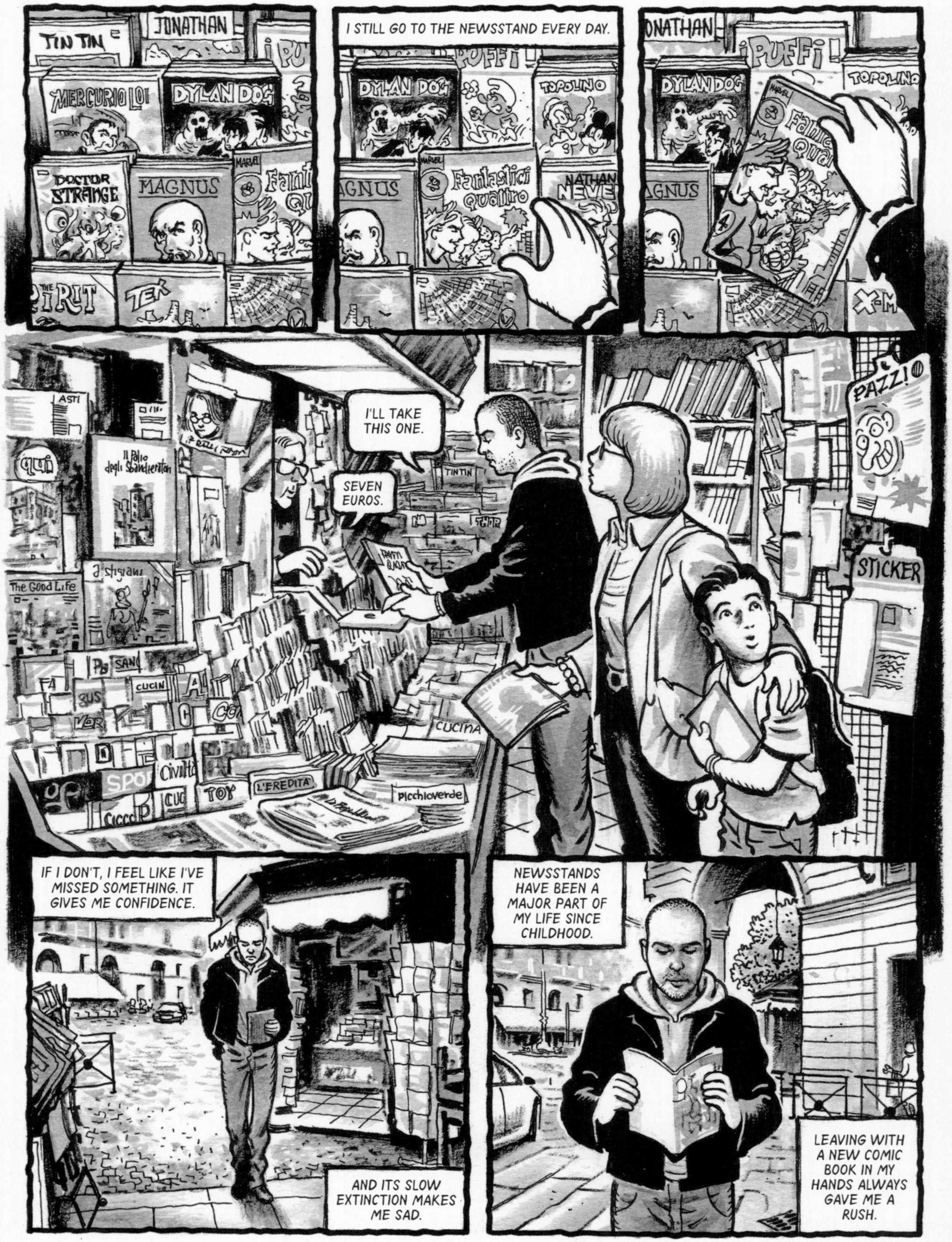
I STILL GO TO THE NEWSSTAND EVERY DAY.
I'LL TAKE THIS ONE.
SEVEN EUROS.
IF I DON'T, I FEEL LIKE I'VE MISSED SOMETHING. IT GIVES ME CONFIDENCE.
AND ITS SLOW EXTINCTION MAKES ME SAD.
NEWSSTANDS HAVE BEEN A MAJOR PART OF MY LIFE SINCE CHILDHOOD.
LEAVING WITH A NEW COMIC BOOK IN MY HANDS ALWAYS GAVE ME A RUSH.

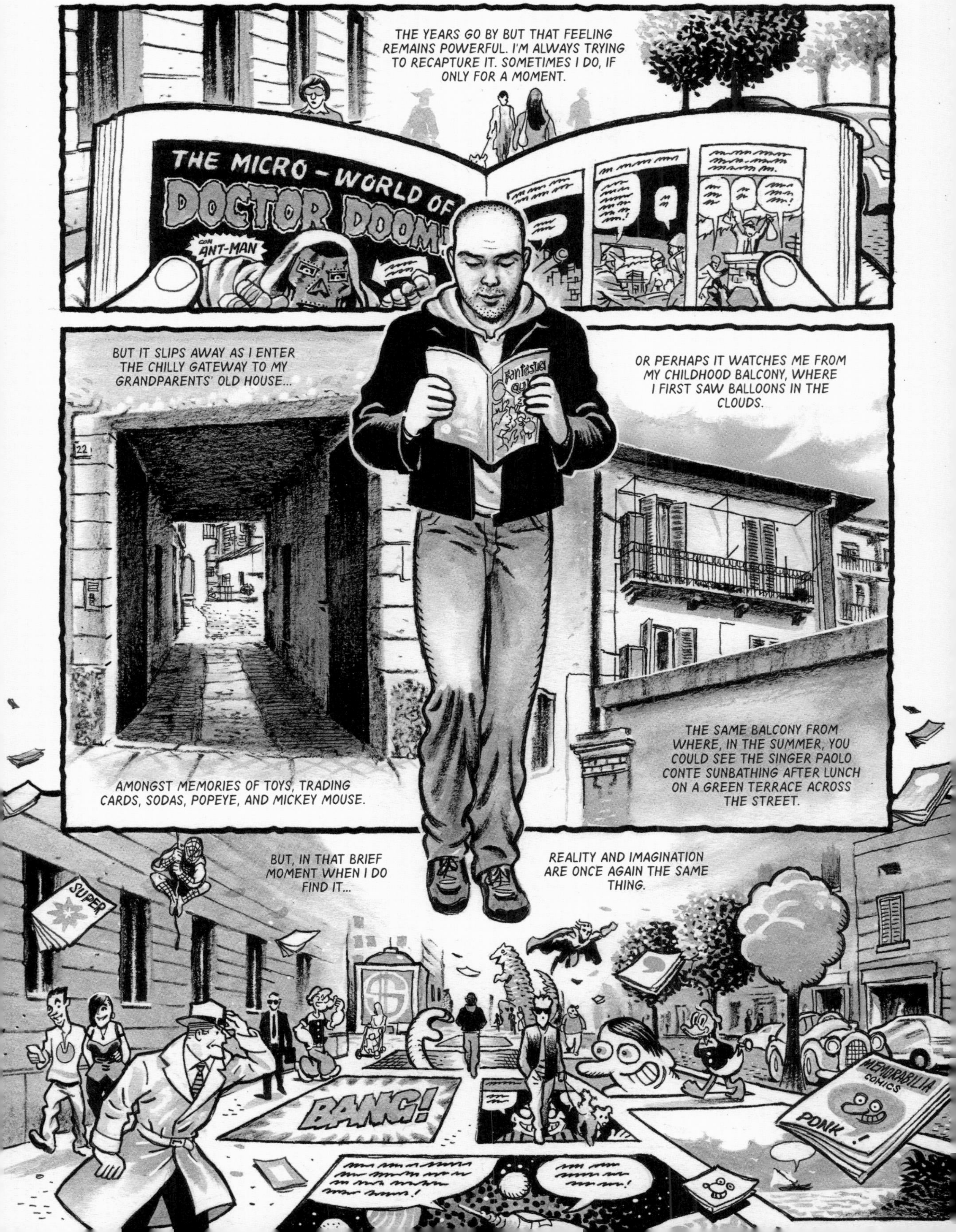
THE YEARS GO BY BUT THAT FEELING REMAINS POWERFUL. I'M ALWAYS TRYING TO RECAPTURE IT. SOMETIMES I DO, IF ONLY FOR A MOMENT.
THE MICRO-WORLD OF DOCTOR DOOM!
CON ANT-MAN
BUT IT SLIPS AWAY AS I ENTER THE CHILLY GATEWAY TO MY GRANDPARENTS' OLD HOUSE...
OR PERHAPS IT WATCHES ME FROM MY CHILDHOOD BALCONY, WHERE I FIRST SAW BALLOONS IN THE CLOUDS.
22
AMONGST MEMORIES OF TOYS, TRADING CARDS, SODAS, POPEYE, AND MICKEY MOUSE.
THE SAME BALCONY FROM WHERE, IN THE SUMMER, YOU COULD SEE THE SINGER PAOLO CONTE SUNBATHING AFTER LUNCH ON A GREEN TERRACE ACROSS THE STREET.
BUT, IN THAT BRIEF MOMENT WHEN I DO FIND IT...
REALITY AND IMAGINATION ARE ONCE AGAIN THE SAME THING.
SUPER
BANG!
MEMORABILIA COMICS
PONK!

STEVE DITKO

STEPHEN J. DITKO (b. Johnstown, Pennsylvania, 1927; d. New York City, 2018) enrolled in the Cartoonists and Illustrators School of New York just after serving in the US Army in Germany, where he drew comics for an army newspaper. He began his career in 1953, as an inker in Joe Simon and Jack Kirby's studio, initially influenced by Mort Meskin's work. At the same time, he began working for Charlton Comics on science fiction, mystery, and horror stories, until tuberculosis kept him away from the drawing table for a year. Upon recovery, he worked for Atlas Comics (before the company became Marvel Comics) on titles such as *Journey Into Mystery*, *Strange Tales*, *Tales to Astonish*, and *Strange Worlds*. Issue #15 of *Amazing Fantasy* featured the first appearance of Spider-Man, cocreated by Ditko and Stan Lee. This—along with the cocreation of Doctor Strange in 1963—was the beginning of a legend, born of Ditko's unique, accomplished style. During those years he and a former schoolmate, the fetish artist Eric Stanton, shared a Manhattan studio where they helped each other meet tight deadlines. Ditko's historic stint at Marvel ended in 1966 due to disagreements with Stan Lee. Beginning in 1967, and throughout the 1970s, Ditko devoted himself alternately to Charlton (which paid lower rates, but afforded him more creative freedom), where he created the Question, the Blue Beetle, and Captain Atom, and DC Comics, where he created the Creeper, Hawk & Dove, and Shade the Changing Man. He also contributed to Jim Warren's *Creepy* and *Eerie* magazines, and created the controversial Mr. A for Wallace Wood's self-published *witzend* magazine. In 1979, Ditko returned to Marvel, working on *Machine Man*, *The Micronauts*, *ROM*, *Speedball*, and other titles until the late 1990s. In 1998, he retired from mainstream comics freelancing, and has since copublished new work with Robin Snyder, his former Charlton editor. Now in his late nineties, he continues to create, and remains as mysterious as ever.

JACK KIRBY

JACOB KURTZBERG (b. New York, New York, 1917; d. Thousand Oaks, California, 1994) made his comics debut during the 1930s under several different pseudonyms, until he settled on the one that would make him famous. In 1939, the Fleischer Studios hired him as an "in-betweener" for *Popeye* cartoons, but the early growth of the comic book industry led him to the Eisner & Iger Studio, and eventually to a fortuitous meeting with Joe Simon at Fox Comics. The two would partner up to produce work for Timely Comics (forerunner to Marvel Comics, by way of Atlas Comics), where they would cocreate Captain America. During the 1940s Kirby worked for National Comics (soon to be DC Comics) and, after serving in WWII, partnered again with Joe Simon to create the Fighting American and invent the romance comics genre for Crestwood Publications. They even launched their own short-lived comic book company, Mainline Publications. Kirby freelanced for both Atlas and National until he began working exclusively for Atlas on sci-fi and supernatural titles, which led him to collaborate on the first issue of *Fantastic Four* with Stan Lee—thereby (inadvertently) revolutionizing the industry. During the 1960s, Lee and Kirby conceptualized and defined the fledgling Marvel Universe with the creation of characters such as Thor, the Hulk, Iron Man, the X-Men, and many others. After this golden decade of creative and commercial success, in which he refined his powerful, dynamic art style, Kirby grew dissatisfied with how Marvel treated him and migrated to DC Comics in 1970. As writer and artist, Kirby gave life to his "Fourth World" saga, which tied together titles such as *New Gods*, *Mister Miracle*, and *Forever People*, in addition to working on series like *OMAC*, *Kamandi*, and *The Demon*. In 1976, he returned to Marvel for one last time, working on *The Eternals*, *Captain America*, *Machine Man*, *Devil Dinosaur*, *Black Panther*, and an unforgettable adaptation of Stanley Kubrick's film *2001: A Space Odyssey*. Further dissatisfaction with Marvel (and comics) pushed him into the animation and film industries for much of the 1980s. His last creative efforts in comics, during the 1980s, included *Captain Victory and the Galactic Rangers* and *Silver Star* for Pacific Comics, and *The Hunger Dogs* for DC Comics. Twenty years after his death, his work still remains an unattainable exemplar of energy and creative power in the eyes of many young artists and fans.

WALLACE WOOD

WALLACE A. WOOD (b. Menahga, Minnesota, 1927; d. Los Angeles, California, 1981) read and drew comics during his childhood. During WWII he was drafted into the US Navy as a paratrooper. Ater he was discharged, he began attending the Minneapolis School of Art, before moving to New York City in 1948. There, he enrolled in Burne Hogarth's Cartoonists and Illustrators School (which is now the School of Visual Arts) for a short time before trying his hand as a freelancer. After many rejections, he managed to get hired by Will Eisner's studio as an assistant on *The Spirit*. After a stint at Fox Comics, he eventually found his way to EC Comics, where he reunited with several cartoonists he'd met earlier at different studios, including John Severin, Harvey Kurtzman, and Will Elder. By 1950, Wood began to make a name for himself, working exclusively for EC. His painstakingly rich art for EC's sci-fi, horror, adventure, war, and suspense stories—on now-mythical titles like *Weird Science*, *Tales from the Crypt*, *Two-Fisted Tales*, and *Shock SuspenStories*—helped make a name for EC as the best publisher in the business. EC also published *Mad*, which, supervised by Kurtzman, allowed Wood to showcase his humorous side. Wood eventually returned to Will Eisner's

trademark character, drawing a legendary sequence of "Outer Space Spirit" stories. Wood was unstoppable at this point, churning out covers and illustrations for *Galaxy Science Fiction*, issues of *Daredevil* for Marvel, and comics for DC, Warren, Avon, Charlton, and Gold Key, as well as working on newspaper strips (*Bucky's Christmas Caper*), trading cards (*Mars Attacks!*), advertising campaigns, and much more. In 1965 he cofounded the unlucky Tower Comics company, where he oversaw the *T.H.U.N.D.E.R. Agents* and *Dynamo* titles. Tower Comics led soon to *witzend*, one of the first independent comics magazines that afforded authors complete creative freedom and ownership of their work. During the 1970s he worked on *The Wizard King* trilogy and, helped by many assistants, was still active in the field until his death in 1981.

WILL EISNER

WILLIAM ERWIN EISNER (b. New York, 1917—Lauderdale Lakes, 2005), a Jewish immigrants' son, studied at the DeWitt Clinton High School and the Art Students League of New York. In 1936, he debuted in the then-rising world of comics together with publisher Jerry Iger, opening the Eisner & Iger Studio, producing comic books for publishers like Fox Comics, Fiction House, and Quality Comics. From the latter he got an offer to create a character of his own for the Sunday supplements of newspapers, and he was eager to enter the ever-growing comics market. So, in 1940, the masked detective The Spirit—Eisner's most famous creation—was born. Translated and reprinted all over the world, *The Spirit* ennobled the language of comics using brilliant experimentation and introducing more adult topics. After Eisner was drafted into the US Army in 1942, his character enjoyed the creativity of Eisner colleagues such as Jules Feiffer, Jack Cole, and Lou Fine. But the uniform didn't stop Eisner; he worked for military magazines such as *Army Motors* and, above all, *PS Magazine*, on which he collaborated until 1971. Upon his return to civilian life, he resumed work on *The Spirit* until 1952, when his American Visuals Corporation began producing instructional materials

for the US government along with other related agencies and businesses. By the end of the '70s he came back to the comics with *A Contract with God*, one of the first examples of the modern graphic novel, followed by many other titles, such as *A Life Force*, *The Building*, *Dropsie Avenue*, *To the Heart of the Storm*, and *The Plot*. His teaching years at the School of Visual Arts in New York led him to write two books about comics, *Comics and Sequential Art* and *Graphic Storytelling and Visual Narrative*. Eisner is considered one of the most important comics creators ever and a key influence for many of today's comics creators. The Eisner Award, one of the most prestigious prizes of American comic art, was named in his honor.

RICHARD CORBEN

RICHARD VANCE CORBEN (b. Anderson, 1940) got a degree in Fine Arts at Kansas City Art Institute in 1965. After working as a professional animator, he began producing underground comics for titles such as *Grim Wit*, *Slow Death*, *Skull*, *Rowlf*, *Fever Dreams*, and his own anthology, *Fantagor*. In 1970 he began illustrating horror and sci-fi stories for Warren Publishing, which ran in the pages of *Creepy*, *Eerie*, *Vampirella*, and *1984*, while also coloring several installments of Eisner's *The Spirit*. In 1975 he sent some of his works to the editors of the French magazine, *Mètal Hurlant*, who quickly enlisted him for the American edition of the mag, *Heavy Metal*. There Corben published his celebrated fantasy saga, *Den*, named after a character taken from an early animated short of his; *Den* was later featured in the animated *Heavy Metal* film. In 1976, *Bloodstar* was published, one of the first comic books that self-identified as a "graphic novel" in its introduction. Corben's peculiar graphic and coloring techniques, partially derived from animation, already made him unique. Comics writers such as Bruce Jones, Harlan Ellison, and Jan Strnad began writing stories for him, producing several books, including *Vic & Blood*, *Jeremy Brood*, *Arabian Nights*, and *Son of a Mutant World*, among them. From 1986 to 1994 he ran Fantagor Press, his own publishing house, while producing countless illustrations, album covers (*Bat Out of Hell* by Meat Loaf), and movies (*Phantom of the Paradise* by Brian de Palma.) In the early 2000s he worked with various comics writers for DC, Marvel, Dark Horse and IDW on several regular series, miniseries, and one-shots, including *Hellblazer*, *Ghost Rider*, *Hellboy*, *Hulk*, *Cage*, *The Punisher*, *Aliens*, *Starr the Slayer*, *Bigfoot*, *Conan*, as well as memorable comics adaptation of tales by Edgar Allan Poe, H.P. Lovecraft, and William Hope Hodgson. After winning two Eisner Awards, in 2012 he was included in the Will Eisner Comic Book Hall of Fame, and, in 2015, in the Ghastly Awards Hall of Fame. Still active, he recently produced the *Ragemoor* miniseries, written by Jan Strnad, and *Rat God*, both published by Dark Horse.

Written and illustrated by Sergio Ponchione

Editor and Associate Publisher: Eric Reynolds
Book Design: Sergio Ponchione and Justin Allan-Spencer
Production: Paul Baresh
Translated from Italian by Diego Ceresa
Publisher: Gary Groth

FANTAGRAPHICS BOOKS INC.
7563 Lake City Way NE
Seattle, Washington, 98115
www.fantagraphics.com

ISBN 978-1-68396-148-2
Library of Congress Control Number 2018936475

First edition: November 2018
Printed in China

The first 27 pages of Memorabilia originally appeared in the comic book *DKW—Ditko Kirby Wood* (Fantagraphics, 2014).

"The Mysterious Steve" is in part inspired by an article by Reed Tucker, "The Secret Hero of Spider-Man," that appeared in the *New York Post* (March 7, 2012).

"Wood & Me" contains some biographical information taken from *Wally's World* by Steve Starger and J. David Spurlock (Vanguard Productions, 2006).

Selected Bibliography:

Strange and Stranger: The World of Steve Ditko by Blake Bell
(Fantagraphics Books, 2008)

Kirby: King of Comics by Mark Evanier (Abrams, 2008)

Against the Grain: Mad Artist Wally Wood by Bhob Stewart
(TwoMorrows Publishing, 2003)

Creepy Presents Richard Corben by Richard Corben
(Dark Horse Comics, 2012)

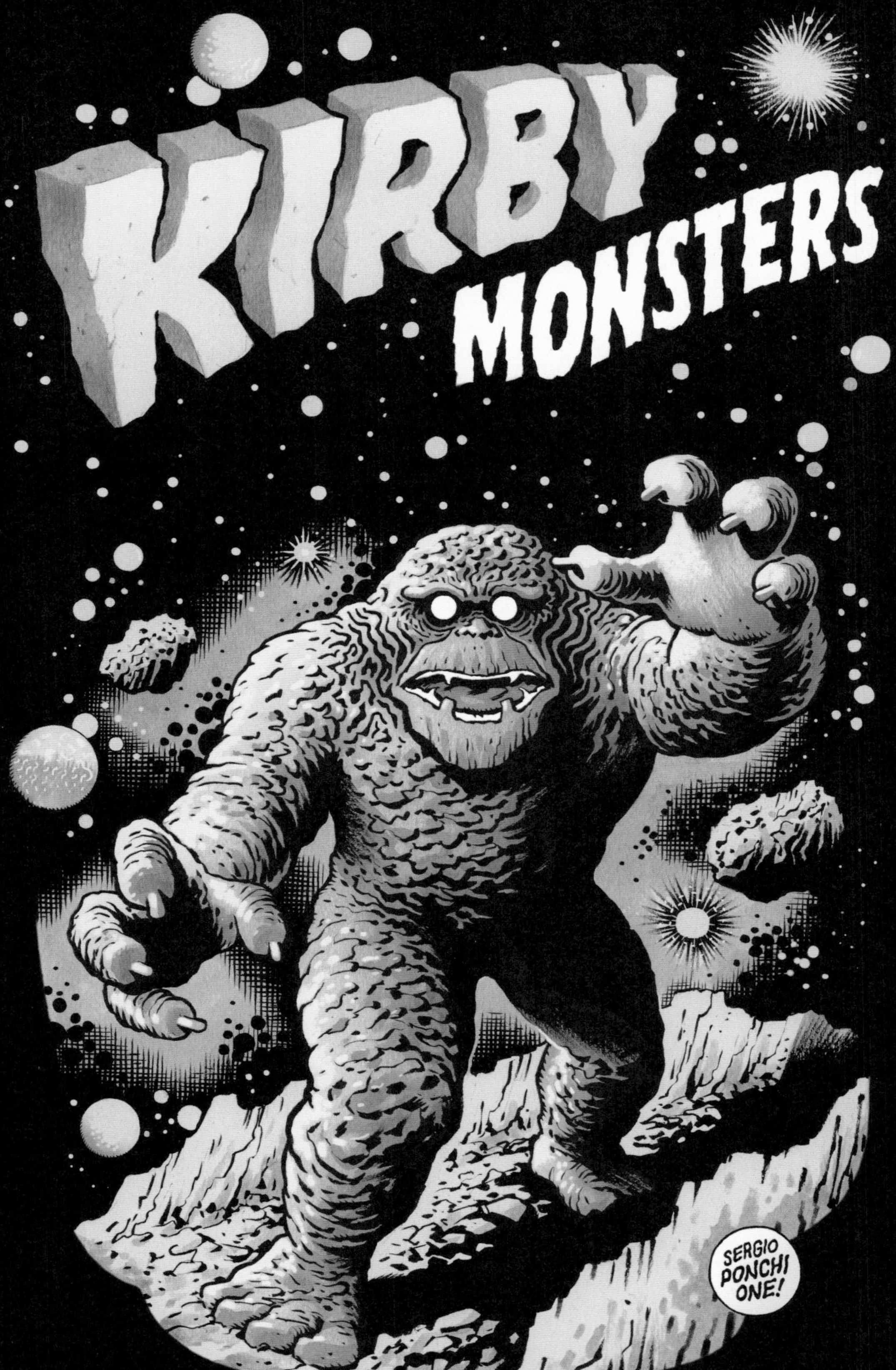
KIRBY
MONSTERS
SERGIO
PONCHI
ONE!